Melting Steel

C.M. Seabrook

MELTING STEEL

MELTING STEEL

Prologue

Henry

Twenty Years Ago…

I swing my sword at my enemy, ramming it into his heart, and letting out a loud cheer as his blood and guts spill on the ground.

"You're so weird." Abby rolls her eyes at me, then turns and starts towards her house where the Sullivans are hosting their annual summer barbeque. She calls over her shoulder when she's halfway up the hill. "Race you."

"Not fair," I shout back.

I'm about to chase after her when I hear a woman crying from somewhere behind the large bushes that line the driveway.

"You can't be here," a man shouts.

"I need you. Your children need–"

"Shut up." There's a sharp slapping sound followed by a cry of pain. "Keep your voice down."

My chest tightens as I push my way through the bushes in order to see better. I know I shouldn't be here. I'm not allowed past the big trees and I'd be in a lot of trouble if my dad found out I was spying on grown-ups. But the woman sounds scared.

"If you don't leave now, I swear I'll stop payments completely." The man has his back to me, but I know his voice. *Mr. Sullivan*, Abby's dad. I don't like him. He's always making Abby and her mom cry, and now he's hurting the lady.

"John, please." The woman's belly is big, like she's going to have a baby. She reaches out to touch him, but he pushes her away.

I move closer and a couple of the branches snap. Mr. Sullivan looks over his shoulder in my direction, but I don't think he sees me.

"You need to leave." He grabs the woman by the arm and pulls her roughly towards an old brown car that looks out of place among the line of black limos.

I look down at my wooden sword. I should do something. Make him stop hurting the lady. That's what a knight would do. But Mr. Sullivan is scary when he gets mad, and I'm already in trouble for feeding ants to my sister's Baby Alive doll.

I swallow hard. Feeling like a coward.

A few feet away, a young girl peeks her head around the nearest tree, then quickly hides.

"Hey," I say, but not too loudly, in case Mr. Sullivan hears me. "Wait."

I race after her when she runs to another tree, this one not big enough to hide behind.

When I catch up to her, she looks at me, eyes wide. They're blue, like Abby's, only paler. And her lashes are long and dark like her hair.

She chews her lip, and wipes her eyes with the back of her arm. She's too little to be on her own. Maybe she's lost. But she doesn't look like she belongs to anyone at the party. Her t-shirt is stained and her pink running shoes have holes in the toes.

I glance back in the direction I came from. Maybe she belongs to the woman.

"Is that your mom with Mr. Sullivan?" I whisper, just loud enough for her to hear.

She nods. There are large bruises on her arms and legs, and a faded yellow one on her cheek. Something inside me starts to hurt when I look at them. I have bruises too, from falling off my bike. But hers look different, like someone hurt her on purpose.

"I'm Henry." I move toward her slowly. "What's your name?"

"Keeley." She looks down at the ground and her hair falls over her face.

"How old are you?"

"Six."

"I'm eight, but I'll be nine next month," I say proudly, standing taller.

I should go back to the house. I'll get in trouble if someone finds me here. But I don't want to leave the girl. I can tell she's scared.

The woman is crying loudly again and Mr. Sullivan is really angry now. I've never heard anyone sound so angry, not even my mom when I cut my sister's hair.

"Why's Mr. Sullivan mad at your mom?"

She shrugs her shoulders, and when she blinks, tears run down her cheeks.

"It's okay. I'll stay with you."

When she sits down on the grass, I sit beside her, my back against the tree, and place my sword on my knees.

We sit in silence, and I see her shrink back when Mr. Sullivan yells again.

"Have you ever seen a real dragon?" That's what he sounds like when he yells – a dragon roaring. And just as scary.

The girl shakes her head.

"I have," I say proudly, even though it's not really true. I don't care that Abby says they're just pretend, I believe they're real. And one day I'm going to go on a quest like the knights in my books and find one. "They're big and scary. And they make an awful noise." I growl in my throat and she giggles. "But if you're brave, and your heart is good, you can defeat it"–I jump up, and swing my sword in the air– "with one blow to the heart."

"I don't have a sword."

"Girls don't need swords." I stand taller and puff out my chest. "They have knights to protect them."

"I want to be a knight, too."

"Only boys can be knights."

"Oh." Her mouth turns down in a frown.

I sit down beside her and pull a dandelion from the grass beside me, handing it to her.

"But I can be your champion."

"What's a champion?"

"A knight who protects a lady. We learned all about it at school. We had to do a report on it and mine was the best. You give me a token, like a ribbon or something, then I fight the bad guys for you."

She chews on her lip, then reaches down and unties one of her shoelaces.

"Like this?" She hands me the dirty lace.

"Yeah." I take it and shove it in my pocket, feeling proud of myself. She's not crying anymore. "Now I'm sworn to protect you."

"From bad men." She glances over to where the woman and Mr. Sullivan are fighting.

"Yep," I say, even though the thought makes my stomach hurt. I look back at her and make claws with my fingers. "And from dragons."

She giggles, then throws her arms around my neck. "Thank you."

I don't jerk away from her like I do when Abby tries to hug me.

"Keeley," the woman's panicked cry echoes across the parking lot.

She stands quickly. "I have to go."

"Here," I say, handing her my sword. I don't know why I do it, but she seems to need it more than me. "I'm getting a new one for my birthday anyways."

"I can't." She tries to give it back.

"Keep it." I point to the three letters that I'd cut into the handle of the sword with my pocket knife. "H.W.C. That's my name. So you'll remember me."

"Keeley. Get over here right now," the woman screeches. I can see her face now, red and swollen from crying.

Keeley hugs me again, then runs off, darting between the cars, taking the sword with her.

I hope it'll keep her safe – *Until I find her again.*

Chapter 1

Keeley

"Mr. Tall, Dark and Perfect is watching you again," Britt says, leaning against the bar, waiting while I fill her order.

I roll my eyes at the nickname she's given the hottie at table twenty-two, and shrug, trying my best not to look in *his* direction. But I can feel the pull of his gaze, and a small shiver races down my spine.

I'm used to men ogling. Part of working at The Cocoon Nightclub means being harassed nightly by over-plumed peacocks tossing their daddy's money around like they're Donald Trump, Jr.

But there's something different about this one. And it's not just that he's pure, panty-soaking, sex on a stick, of male hotness. He's got the whole smoldering, "I can fulfill every dark fantasy you've ever dreamt about," thing going on.

The intensity of his gaze unnerves me, burns through me. There's no emotion in his eyes, just raw, carnal desire.

He quirks an eyebrow when he catches me staring.

Shit.

The guy knows he's hot. I don't begrudge him for it. It's not like he's never looked in a mirror. But it's the arrogance of his posture, the slight tilt of his head, the small smirk that plays across his kissable lips that warn me whatever he's after is anything but harmless flirting.

When he starts towards the bar, my pulse speeds up, and every nerve in my body screams – *run.*

"Keeley?" Britt's terse voice snaps me back to reality.

"Sorry." My cheeks are warm, my voice breathless. I pour two tumblers of Glenfiddich and turn my back to the bar.

Deep breath and release.

A mix of high-pitched whining and pulsating throbs, beat steadily through the large room, and I can feel my heartrate pumping with it.

I sense him behind me. Like a sexual magnet, I can't resist.

Get a grip, Keeley.

My hormones are on overdrive. But that's what I get for going on a man-fast for the last eighteen months. *A fast I don't plan on breaking anytime soon.* My life is complicated enough. I don't need an extra dose of testosterone screwing it up more than it already is.

"Have we met before?" A dark, rich voice carries over the music, making me shiver.

I steel my spine and turn. But I'm not prepared for the impact of meeting him face to face. My breath leaves me in a swoosh and I suddenly feel like my world just got a million times smaller. All the noises around us, the voices, music, seems into nothing.

The only thing I'm aware of is *him*.

His features are strong, angular, *masculine*. Dark lashes frame coal black eyes that smolder with an intensity that makes my entire body burn. Even with my four-inch stilettos, the man towers me by a good six inches.

He runs a hand through his dark hair, mussing the waves slightly. But the disheveled look only makes him hotter.

I've been around "bad boys" my entire life. But this man is a whole new category of bad. He has heartbreaker written all over him. And I can tell by the way he's looking at me that he has every intention of making me his next conquest.

Not happening, buddy.

"Do you want something?" My tone is snappier than I intended, but I can't help feeling agitated by his very presence.

He tilts his chin, the corner of his lips twitching up, and he continues to study me as if I'm some kind of exotic prey.

Despite the wetness between my legs, and the overpowering need to let him consume me, I clench my teeth, place my hands on the edge of the bar, and narrow my eyes.

"Look, if you're wanting some kind of show, there's a strip club a couple blocks east of here. You might have better luck there."

I bite my tongue, knowing if my manager heard the way I just spoke to a customer, I'd be back on my ass searching for another job.

When will I learn to keep my mouth shut?

For a moment, he looks taken aback, then he starts to laugh, deep and throaty. A sound that makes my knees go weak.

Damn him, and his perfectly coiffed hair that's begging me to reach out and brush my fingers through it.

"You remind me of someone." He leans against the bar casually, one hand in the pocket of his slacks. Under the expensive suit and white button-down, I can tell the man's body is hard as granite.

"Lucky me." I have to physically restrain myself from rolling my eyes. At least twice a night I have some drunken asshole comparing me to Megan Fox or Olivia Wilde. It's the dark hair and blue eyes. I don't see it. But the skanky, silver sequin dress the club makes the wait staff and bartenders wear doesn't help.

"Do you want a drink or not?" *Why am I being such a bitch?* I deal with guys like him every night, but for some reason I've let him get under my skin. I bite my lip, and breathe in through my nose. "Can I get you something?"

"Gin and tonic." He unbuttons his jacket and sits down on one of the stools across from me.

Everything about him, his clothes, the way he moves, is precise, calculated. *Dangerous.*

I take his glass and place it in the rinser, feeling my cheeks start to burn. What is it about this guy?

Our fingers touch when he reaches out to take the drink I place in front of him.

Real or imagined zaps of energy explode through my hand. I pull back too quickly, and the man actually chuckles.

Prick.

Britt has come back for a new order and is staring open-mouthed between us. I give her a look that says shut it.

"I'm Henry."

"Henry?" I say, raising an eyebrow. Not the name I would have picked for him. But in a way it suits him. Stuck up. Arrogant.

He gives me a half-smile, one side quirking up more than the other.

"It was my grandfather and father's name." His fingers, which I can't help notice are exceptionally long, casually tap the solid black marble counter.

Focus, Keeley.

"So you're Henry the third," I mock, shaking my head. "Sounds about right. Wasn't he the guy who killed all of his wives?"

"That was the eighth." He smiles, eyes sparkling with humor. "The third was a much better guy."

"I'm sure," I say, placing the last of Britt's order on her tray.

"You know, it's common courtesy to give your name in return." He takes a sip of his drink, dark eyes never wavering from me.

I ignore him, turning my back.

"Her name's Keeley," Britt says, giving me an impish grin, before taking her tray and sauntering back into the crowd.

Traitor.

15

"Keeley." My name practically drips off his tongue, like he's tasting it, and my entire body responds.

I glare at him, moving down the bar to help another customer. I take my time, hoping that he'll take a hint and leave.

He doesn't.

"You're still here." I give an exasperated sigh.

"Are you always this good-natured?" His words drip with sarcasm, but the banter is light, as if he enjoys my snarky remarks.

"Are you always this pushy?"

He leans closer, eyes dark with intent. "Only when I want something."

A tremor of anticipation rolls through me.

I cross my arms over my chest, which drives my breasts higher, exposing more cleavage. When I see his gaze lower, I quickly drop my hands to my side.

"Look. I'm sure this whole thing"–With both hands, I motion to the perfection that is him– "you've got going on works well enough with other women. But I'm not interested, so why don't you head back to your table, and I'll send a waitress over to help you."

"I want *you* to help me." One dark brow cocks, and he continues to smirk at me, like I'm there for his entertainment.

I swear my nipples harden under his lust-filled gaze.

Damn him. I need to get away. I signal Jess at the other end of the bar and tell him I'm going to the back to get some more limes. His brows furrow when he looks down at the full container of citrus fruit in front of me, but nods anyways.

My cheeks are burning. Hell, my whole body is on fire when I push through the door that leads to the refrigerator room. I'm grateful for the cool burst of air when it hits my over-heated body.

I lean against the cool wall and close my eyes. But I can't block out the man's face, the promise of pleasure in his dark eyes. Images of corded muscles pinning me to the wall, my legs wrapped around his narrow waist as he thrusts into me, hard and fast, until I'm crying out his name and giving into all his dark, dirty demands.

Shit.

My vibrator is definitely going to get a workout tonight.

The rough fabric of my dress rubs against my hard nipples, making me groan deep in my throat. I run my hand over my breasts, trying to ease the discomfort, but it only makes it worse.

My own touch isn't enough.

"Need some help?"

My body jolts and my eyes shoot open. I nearly trip over a crate of lemons as I try to regain my composure.

How long has he been there watching me?

"You aren't allowed back here." My voice cracks on the last word.

He saunters towards me, a grin playing on those luscious lips.

"Do you want me to leave?" He moves with power, confidence, like he owns the place...like he owns *me*. "Say the word and I'll walk away."

I swallow hard, knowing what he's offering, and knowing I'm in no position to handle it. But then, it's only sex, and it's been so long.

"If someone found you here, I'd lose my job."

"No one's coming back." The certainty in his tone makes me wonder if he made sure of it. He leans into me, and the scruff on his cheek rubs against my jaw. "Tell me you don't want me."

"I...I don't..."

His hands wrap around my waist, pulling me towards him, his hard erection presses into my belly. Even through the thick material, I can tell he's big – *huge.*

My body molds to his and a chill races down my spine. A wave of arousal soaks my panties and I clench my thighs. I need this. *Crave it.*

I could let him take me. Here. Now. I've never done anything so brazen. No one-night stands. No sex with random strangers. But there's something about *him* that has my defenses shattered.

Shouting from the other side of the doorway breaks the spell.

"I have to go." I move past him quickly, pushing through the door, and ignoring the look Britt gives me.

"Get off me." I know that voice.

Jax. All two-hundred and twenty pounds of muscle and tattoos pushes past the two, much smaller and seemingly terrified bouncers.

Shit, shit, shit.

This can't be happening.

I think about ducking behind the bar, but his eyes lock on me, and I know there's nowhere to hide.

He storms towards me, eyes glassed over and wild.

A coldness settles in the pit of my stomach. *This is the danger I'm used to.*

Damn him to hell. I need this job.

"Where is he?" Jax growls, pupils small pinpricks from whatever he's using.

I move around the bar quickly, hoping to make as little a scene as possible, but already there are a handful of curious faces watching us.

"You can't be here." I clench my jaw, and try to pull him in the direction of the back, but he doesn't budge.

"The little bastard stole from me. I want my money." His hands wrap around my upper arm in a bruising grip. He leans down so that his hot breath warms my cheek, and growls, "And the drugs."

"I don't know what you're talking about."

"I've got witnesses that saw your brother leaving my apartment this afternoon."

Damn it, Drew. I love my brother, would do anything for him, but messing with Jax isn't just stupid, it's deadly.

"Whatever he took, I'll pay you back."

His mouth twists into a scowl.

"Damn right you will." Blond hair hangs in greasy dreadlocks around his face. His eyes are sunken in, and there are lines around his eyes and mouth that make him look older than twenty-seven.

Drugs and alcohol destroyed the man I once cared about. Made him into the monster that stands before me now. I could forgive him if he hadn't dragged Drew into his own personal hell.

"I had more than ten thousand dollars in that bag. Either the kid gets it back to me tonight—" He trails his finger down my throat. "Or it'll be on both your heads. Understand?"

I don't see Henry approach, but I can feel him. And I can tell Jax does too, because his grip tightens on my arm and his focus is momentarily redirected.

Even from a few feet away I can see the tension in Henry's body. He's taken off his jacket, and rolled his sleeves above his forearms. Everything about his stance says that he's ready to fight.

Is he freaking kidding?

"Let go of the lady." Henry's voice is deep, commanding, and for a split second, Jax's grip loosens.

"Lady?" Jax laughs, squeezing tighter. "She ain't no lady, buddy." He lowers his head and rasps into my ear, "Are you, darling?"

"Please. Just leave." Despite the fear raging inside me, I'm able to keep some semblance of control to my voice, that is until I see Henry move towards us. He's decided to play the white knight, which is a pretty stupid move, considering Jax outweighs him by a good thirty pounds. "Shit."

Jax is eyeing him now. I've seen the look a hundred times. He's ready and willing for a fight. And with whatever shit that's he's high on, there's no saying how far he'll take it.

"Walk away," I warn. My words directed at Henry. "I can handle this."

"You heard her, asshole."

Instead of running, or at least backing down like any sane person would do, Henry rolls his neck, a slight grin curving his lips. "I heard her ask you to leave."

"You know this clown?" Jax sneers.

"No."

"Yes. And I suggest you take your hands off of her. *Now.*"

New fear builds inside me when Jax releases me.

A growl that sounds more animal than human rumbles in Jax's throat, and I see the moment he decides to charge. He moves quickly. One large meaty arm snaps back preparing to strike. He's going to kill him.

I cringe and close my eyes, unable to watch the train wreck that's about to happen. I just pray Jax doesn't do too much damage to the guy's face. It's a good face. *A really good face.*

Bar stools crash, people scream and there's a series of grunts, followed by shouting and chaos.

My eyes are only closed for a few seconds, but when I open them, Jax is on the floor, barely conscious.

Holy shit.

The minute Henry's eyes lock with mine, his lips twitch up in an arrogant grin.

Even though I try, I can't look away. I've never been so annoyed, and so fricking turned on at the same time before.

21

My manager is screaming orders, and the two bouncers who were all but useless are trying to pick Jax up and maneuver him through the back entrance. If Jax was pissed before, he's going to be hell bent on destroying me now.

I'm sure Tall, Dark, and Sexy had every intention on protecting me, but he's just gone and made things a hell of a lot worse.

"You okay?" My unwanted hero strolls towards me, and I can tell by the look in his eyes that he expects me to fall to his feet and thank him. *Not going to happen.*

"I told you to walk away."

Dark eyes lock on me, and I shudder at what I see in his gaze.

Irritation.

Concern.

Lust.

Yeah, this guy is definitely trouble.

"You should have minded your own business."

"And let him hurt you?"

"He wouldn't have hurt me." Even to my own ears, the lie is unconvincing.

"He already did." His knuckles caress the bare skin of my arm, where bruises are already forming.

For a moment I let my guard drop. Despite the warning bells going off in my head, there's something about this guy that makes me feel safe, protected. *A fool's fantasy.* No one can protect me, but me.

He's a stranger. And there's nothing safe about him. I shake my head and take a small step back, so that he's no longer touching me, and swallow past the lump that's suddenly formed in my throat.

"I can take care of myself," I mumble.

"Not as well as I can take care of you." The innuendo in his words isn't lost on me. He leans down, not breaking eye contact. His voice is low and full of promise when he asks, "How long has it been since someone has taken care of you, Keeley?"

I shiver, every nerve in my body firing at once.

"I have a perfectly good vibrator that works just fine." *Shit. Did I just say that?*

His head tilts back and he laughs. Without warning, a muscular arm wraps around my waist, and his other hand snakes behind my neck, fingers twisting in my hair with just enough force to pull my head back so that I'm looking at him.

"Trust me, sweetheart. A vibrator is no match for the real thing."

My body buzzes with anticipation, and I know he's right.

"Come back to my place and I'll show you."

Yes. "No."

There's humor in his eyes. And I can tell he's not about to back down. His type never does.

I need to get away from him before I do something stupid. I push against his chest, and with some hesitation, he releases me. The second our contact breaks, I regret pushing him away.

"You want me to thank you?" I glare up at him. "I'm probably going to lose my job because of you."

As if on cue, my manager approaches. His eyes are bulging, cheeks bright red, and his forehead is shiny with sweat. I know before he says the words that my prediction is about to come true.

"You're done." He points a stubby finger at me. "Get your things and leave."

I don't even try arguing. What's the point?

Instead, I turn all my pent up emotions on the dark-eyed devil in front of me, and with all the animosity I can muster, I bite out one single word, "Thanks."

Chapter 2

Henry

A firm hand smacks my shoulder as the raven-haired little minx turns on her heels and stalks off.

"Nice left hook you got there." Asher Harrison, my business colleague and soon to be brother-in-law, gives a few air punches in my direction. He's been drinking steadily for the past four hours and he's starting to get sloppy. "I used to box in college. We should jump in the ring sometime."

I've never liked the man, but for Becca I've been trying to put my distaste behind me. That's why I'm here tonight, at his so-called Bachelor party. *Trying* to be civil. It isn't easy. The more time I spend with the guy, the more I get a gut-wrenching feeling that the bastard is nothing but trouble.

Speaking of trouble, I scan the club, searching for Keeley, but she's disappeared.

Damn it.

Lush lips. Blue eyes rimmed with thick dark lashes. A sexy mass of black hair begging for a man's fingers to tangle in.

Keeley. Even her name makes my cock hard.

The woman is gorgeous. But it's more than that. Something I can't put my finger on. The moment those irresistible eyes locked on me, I had the overwhelming urge to hunt, possess, and ultimately to make her *mine*.

She made it clear she isn't interested. But I felt the way she trembled under my touch, saw her eyes widen in anticipation. She wants me, she just doesn't know it yet.

I chuckle under my breath.

Challenge accepted.

There's still a chance I can catch her before she leaves.

I feel like shit that she lost her job, but there was no way in hell I was letting that prick hurt her.

I've seen firsthand what low-level scum like that bastard are capable of.

The room suddenly feels smaller as unwanted memories and regrets tighten my chest.

Abby.

It hits me suddenly. Like a fucking sledgehammer across the head. That's who Keeley reminds me of. *Shit.* I pinch the bridge of my nose and close my eyes, seeing the two women in my head. Abby was blonde, with a slighter, more fragile build. But the similarities are there, in the delicate bone structure, the large, almost haunting blue eyes.

No wonder I reacted so possessively.

"I have to be in the office early tomorrow." I grab my jacket from the barstool, needing to clear my head.

"Don't go." Asher's arm flings over my shoulder, causing the amber liquid to slosh over the rim of his glass. "We're heading to The Doll House. Come with us."

If I weren't repulsed by his suggestion, I'd probably laugh. It's the same strip club Keeley mentioned earlier. It's not that I don't appreciate the female form. Hell, I fucking worship it. But I'm not into paying someone to take their clothes off.

I peel Asher's arm off my shoulder. "I'll pass."

"Your loss, man."

Leaving Asher with the group of clowns he came with, I stop the pretty, redheaded waitress that told me Keeley's name.

"She's gone. Left a few minutes ago." The woman gives me a wicked smile. "But I get off in twenty minutes if you want to wait."

Any other night I'd probably take her up on her offer, but not tonight. Not when both Abby and Keeley's faces keep flashing across my vision like a fucking kaleidoscope.

I exit the club and wait for the valet to return my car, grateful for the cool sting of air as it hits my lungs. I can't help but shake the feeling that I know her, and it's more than just the similarities between her and Abby.

"Call me back as soon as you get this." A woman's panicked voice carries from the shadows about twenty feet away.

I blink, letting my eyes adjust.

Huddled in the corner, nearly hidden behind the large trash canister, her face glows from the soft light of her phone. Her shoulders sag, and she swipes at her cheeks almost angrily. Jeans and an old sweatshirt have replaced the silver sequenced dress, and a pair of Nikes for the stilettos, but even in the darkness I can tell it's her.

What the hell is she doing out here alone?

"Sir." The valet is standing beside me, hand outstretched. My Audi R8 humming like a beautiful symphony behind him.

I place a twenty in the valet's hand, and tell him to wait, knowing something is wrong even before I see the shadow that stalks towards her.

Fuck.

Fury boils in my veins when the hooded figure reaches out and grabs her shoulder.

It takes me mere seconds to reach them. This time I don't wait. I just react. I shove him against the wall, momentarily stunned when I realize it isn't the same man that threatened her in the club.

The kid's hand goes up in surrender, and in the dim light I can see that he's scared shitless.

"Let him go." Keeley smacks at my arm, shouting obscenities that would make an Irishman blush.

"He attacked you."

"I was just coming out to give her, her tip money, man," the kid says, braces flashing in the dim light.

I drop my hands and take a step back.

"What's wrong with you?" Keeley shouts, shoving at my chest.

"Sorry. I thought…" I run my hands through my hair and exhale heavily.

Keeley glares at me, then takes the small roll of bills from the man's hand. "Thanks, James."

"You going to be okay?" James gives me a sideways glance, and I can see in his eyes that he's praying she says yes.

Keeley sighs, shoving the money into the side pocket of her black backpack. "I'll be fine."

He nods, then scurries back in the direction he came from.

She turns on me, blue eyes blazing with anger. "You're stalking me now?"

"I thought you were in trouble."

"You thought wrong." She pushes past me.

I can't explain the tension in my body as I watch her walk away.

"Stop." The command comes out more like a growl than a word.

She goes still, but I can see from the strain in her shoulders that she's fighting whether to run or stay.

I move towards her, and a small shiver goes through her body when I turn her to look at me.

She feels it too. The unmistakable energy between us.

When she looks up at me with those big blue eyes, I know I'm screwed. My fingers itch to touch her, to fuck away the pain I see etched in that beautiful face.

I know I shouldn't give a damn, but I can't help the overpowering need to protect her.

"I have to go. I have to get home." Her voice cracks at the end, betraying her distress.

"I'll drive you." I nudge her chin up with a finger, forcing her to look at me, my mouth a breath away from her lips. I could kiss her, and I know she'd respond, but I also know she'd run afterwards.

She chews on her bottom lip, studying me, waging an internal battle I can't decipher.

Her long dark hair has been pulled up into some kind of knot on the top of her head. My fingers glide over her cheek, then down her neck, toying with a silky strand of hair that's come loose from her bun.

Her cell buzzes and her gaze drops, brows furrowing as she reads the new text message.

"Everything all right?"

"Yes." She looks up at me, giving me those big blue eyes. Eyes that are now filled with uncertainty. "Fine."

I can tell she's lying.

A barrage of emotions hit me. I want to curse her for affecting me like this. But I can't help the voice that screams inside my head.

I need to keep her safe.

"Come on. I'll take you home."

She has no reason to trust me, but I'll be damned if I'm going to leave her out here alone. She's coming with me whether she likes it or not.

After a brief moment of hesitation, she nods.

Some of the tension leaves my body.

I guide her by the elbow to the passenger side door, opening it for her.

She seems suddenly subdued, almost fearful, and it worries me. Something in the text has set her off.

The logical part of my brain reminds me that I barely know her, that she isn't my responsibility. But the Neanderthal part beats its chest, ready to fight anyone who dares threaten her.

I curse under my breath, knowing which one has already won.

Chapter 3

Keeley

My head is spinning and I'm trembling uncontrollably as I get into the car.

Drew's text was clear. *Don't go home. Don't try to find me...I'm sorry.*

Anger overrides the fear I know I should be feeling. Anger at Drew, at Jax, even at the stranger who's done nothing but try to protect me tonight.

What is it with men being self-centered, narcissistic assholes?

I blink back tears and clench my teeth. *I won't cry.*

Henry glances over at me when he gets in the car, brows raised. "Where to?"

Drew said not to go home. It's as much an admission of guilt as anything. I can only assume he knows Jax will search for him there, and when he doesn't find him, it'll be me he takes his rage out on.

I shiver and look away, staring blankly out the window, a cold numbness settling over me.

It won't be the first time I've taken the punishment for something Drew has done.

32

People don't understand why I defend my brother the way I do, but then only a handful of people actually know what we've been through. He's the only family I've got, and I won't let anyone hurt him, even if it means sacrificing myself.

"Keeley?" A warm hand reaches out and touches my leg. "I can't drive you home if I don't know where you live."

"Five-twenty Maple Street." My voice is hoarse, raw, and I hate the emotion I hear in it.

He presses a button and repeats the address. A map pops up on a small screen, and a woman's voice directs him to make a right turn onto Saunders Ave.

We drive a few blocks before either one of us speaks.

"Are you in some kind of trouble?" The way he asks, I know he already assumes I am.

I don't meet his gaze. "I'll be fine."

How many times have I said those words? *I'll be fine.* I wish that I still believed it. But I've been *not* fine for so long, I know that it'll never be true.

He seems to tense, his long fingers tightening around the steering wheel.

Stopped at a red light, he turns his gaze on me, and I can't move, can't turn away.

If my life weren't so fucked up, I'd jump at the chance to spend one night allowing him to fulfill every promise I see in those eyes.

"I can help you find another job," he says, his expression serious. "I own a company–"

"I don't need handouts."

"It isn't a handout. You said yourself it's my fault you got fired. It's the least I can do."

I sigh, shaking my head. The last thing I need is to be indebted to someone like him.

"I can find a job on my own." Another bullshit lie. I've been fired from my last two jobs, and now this one. Who the hell is going to hire me with no references?

He gives me a look that says he doesn't believe me.

We're almost at my apartment, and I have to bite the inside of my cheek to keep my emotions from overwhelming me.

"At least let me give you my number in case you decide–"

"Thank you for the ride." As the car slows, I open the door and jump out, even before we come to a complete stop, knowing if I stay one second longer, I may break and actually accept his offer.

"Keeley, wait." The command in his voice stops me before I can slam the door and take off up the old stone stairs towards my second floor apartment.

A quick glance up and I know someone has been there. The lights are on, and the large fern that usually sits in the windowsill is gone.

I freeze with my hand on the door, already shaking at what I'm going to find. With all the strength I can muster, I give him a small smile, and lie to him one more time, "I'll be fine."

Chapter 4

Henry

I don't know why I follow her. But I do.

The lock on the front door of the building is broken, the plaster walls peeling, and the scent of mildew almost overpowering. The run down brownstone is only four stories, but I only make it to the second floor when I hear Keeley's soft cry of alarm.

A yellow stream of light filters through an open door, and even before I enter the apartment, I know someone has ransacked the place.

"Shit," I mutter, stepping over a broken vase and several scattered magazines. Nothing has been left untouched. Even the old, corduroy couch has been slashed.

Sitting in the corner on an overturned bookshelf, Keeley's face is pale, eyes unfocused. Her gaze drifts up to me, and she blinks several times as if she doesn't really see me.

I move across the room, crouching in front of her, and take her hands in my own.

"Did that asshole from the club do this?"

She lifts her shoulders in a small shrug. "Him. Drew. It doesn't matter. It's all gone."

Who the hell is Drew?

"What were they looking for?"

"Money." Her gaze focuses on me, expression hardening. "Drugs."

I narrow my eyes. "Why would someone be looking for drugs here?"

She drops my hands and stands quickly.

"Are you selling?" I ask, a hard edge to my voice. It's really none of my business, but I can't shake the feeling that I need to protect her. If she's messed up with drugs, it's going to make things a hell of a lot more complicated.

"No." She squares her shoulders and looks me straight in the eyes, and I know she's telling the truth.

With a heavy sigh, she leans down to pick up an overturned plant, then places it on the window sill.

"I'll figure it out." Her words are steel, but there's a vulnerability behind them.

"You need to call the police."

"No."

"Why the hell not?"

She sits down heavily on the torn couch and puts her head in her hands. "Until I know what Drew's done, I can't risk it."

"Drew?" It's the second time she's mentioned the guy. Jealousy tightens my throat.

"My brother." She looks up at me, and my chest constricts at the fear I see in her eyes.

I'm starting to put the pieces together.

"And the guy from the club?"

"Jax."

I grind my back teeth, remembering the way he'd grabbed her.

"He thinks Drew stole from him."

"Did he?"

"I don't know. But if he's using again, then it's possible." Despite what the asshole has done, the danger he's put her in, I can hear the concern in her voice. Concern not for herself, but for her brother. "I have to find him before Jax does."

I have no doubt that whatever she's planning is not only dangerous, but completely idiotic.

If I was smart, I'd get the fuck out of here, now.

Lust wars with self-preservation.

Damn, if I don't want her. But I already know that one taste will never be enough, and the woman has trouble written all over her. She could never be a one-night stand or a casual fuck, and that's all I have room for.

Nothing else. Nothing more.

She doesn't need my help, she already told me that. Not that I believe her. But I need to get away from her before I pull the caveman shit my cock is urging me to do.

I don't even know the woman, but I can safely say I've never felt so fucking possessive over anyone or anything.

It's my nature to control. To fix. Maybe that's all this is.

Maybe.

Whatever it is, I know I've finally found my kryptonite.

Running my hand through my hair, I glance around the apartment, realizing that the lock on the door is broken, the wood frame splintered. She can't stay here.

"You have somewhere you can go for the night?"

She follows my eyes to the door, then shakes her head. "Whoever did this isn't coming back. I've got a lot of work to do cleaning this up, so–"

"Where did you get this?" I bend over to pick up a small wooden sword that's half hidden under the coffee table. I run my fingers over the initials carved into the handle – *H.W.C.*

My initials.

Keeley glances up at me from where she's picking up pieces of broken glass, brows furrowing when she looks at the sword. Emotion flickers across her face, then it's gone, replaced by a cold mask. She shrugs and turns her back to me.

My throat constricts, images of a small, dark-haired little girl, racing through my mind.

No. It can't be.

"What?" She dumps the glass pieces into a wastebasket, then crosses her arms over her chest, blue eyes narrowed on me.

I glance away trying to regain some composure. Was it possible she was my blue-eyed girl? The one I'd sworn to protect. The one I'd been dreaming of for the past twenty years.

Despite the beating I got for persisting otherwise, I knew she was real. That I hadn't made her up.

"Get what you need for the night." The words are spoken before I really think about what I'm suggesting.

Her jaw locks and she studies me for a moment, eyes heavy with mistrust.

"Look." She takes a deep breath, gaze locked on me. "I appreciate you want to help, but this is my problem. I don't even know you."

She's right. We're practically strangers. Christ, I don't even know her last name. But there's no fucking way I'm walking out of this shitty apartment without her.

She's mine. She just doesn't know it yet.

"And what happens when that asshole comes back looking for you?"

She shifts her weight from one foot to the other, and I can tell her mind goes somewhere dark.

"I'll handle him." The confidence that was in her voice moments before is gone. She's scared and she has every reason to be.

I move towards her, ready to use any and all tactics to make her see reason. Sheer force won't work, not with her. If anything, it'll just make her dig her heels in deeper. No, it's time to turn on the charm. Appeal to her feminine needs.

She stiffens slightly when I reach out to stroke a strand of dark hair that's fallen loose from her bun.

"What are you doing?" Her voice cracks slightly on the last word.

A grin pulls at my lips, but I stifle it. I can tell my touch affects her. She's so fucking responsive. I lean in slowly, and wrap my other arm around her waist.

"Come home with me." I brush my thumb across her bottom lip and she instantly parts them for me. *The things I'm going to do with that mouth.*

She shakes her head, but I can tell she's thinking about it. I can feel her resolve fading.

"Just for tonight. There's nothing you can do until morning."

"Just for tonight," she repeats, her gaze focused on my lips.

I lean in slightly and she closes her eyes, clearly anticipating my kiss.

Not yet, sweetheart.

When I finally kiss her, there will be no stopping.

"Go pack a bag."

She nods, and I know I've won.

Chapter 5

Keeley

When he looks at me like that, my panties may as well evaporate. But there's something else behind his gaze, like he actually wants to help me.

Don't be so naïve, Keeley.

He wants one thing from me, and once he gets it, I'll be just another notch on his bedpost.

But at least I'll have the night to figure out what to do. I have no doubt Jax will be back, looking for me.

I keep saying that I don't need his help, but the truth is I'm terrified – for myself, but also for Drew. I made a promise years ago that I'd never let anyone hurt him again, and I've sacrificed everything to make sure no one did.

But I can't protect him from Jax. Not unless I can somehow come up with the money he's stolen.

Ten thousand dollars. Shit. It might as well be a million.

The small envelope I kept taped under the couch is gone. Tip money that I was going to use to pay for this month's rent. It was only five hundred dollars, but it was all I had.

"You have everything you need?" A calloused hand brushes against the bare skin of my arm, sending a wave of heat rushing to my core. And again, the world stops, and nothing but him seems to matter.

I nod, and he places his hand on my lower back, ushering me out of the apartment and down to his car.

The shadows seem to have eyes, and I get the overwhelming sense that we're being watched as he places my bags in the trunk.

He must sense it too, because the muscle in his jaw seems to jump, and his frown deepens.

I focus on keeping my breathing even, but I don't relax until I'm in the car with Henry beside me. It's odd how safe I feel with him. Beyond the sexual magnetism and bad boy good looks, there's something else about him that pulls at the back of my mind – a sense of familiarity like I somehow know him.

The silence between us hangs heavy, until we pull into the private underground parking garage of a luxury high-rise.

"You okay?"

I give a small nod and bite my bottom lip to hide the slight tremble that threatens to expose my nerves.

"Come on. I'll grab your bag."

He guides me into the elevator, and I need to remind myself to breathe when he inserts a key, punches in a code, then presses the top button on the chrome panel.

I can feel his gaze on me, hot and heavy. He hasn't touched me since we left my place, but the heat between us is almost tangible. His intentions are clear, and I'm both excited and terrified at the same time.

"I don't usually do this."

"Do what?" A smile twitches the corners of his mouth.

"Go home with random men."

"I wouldn't judge you if you did." He reaches out and tucks my hair behind my ear, his touch sending shockwaves of pleasure racing down my spine.

"Well, I don't. It's been eighteen months since I've–" I bite my tongue on the awkward confession.

"Since what?" His eyes sparkle with humor, but there's nothing comical about the way his hands trail down the swell of my breasts, then around my back, drawing me towards him. His mouth is inches from mine, his breath warm against my lips.

The man's touch is lethal. My body practically vibrates with need.

"Don't be nervous." The way he watches me, it's like he can read my thoughts.

"I'm not," I lie.

A small bing tells us that we've arrived, and I take a small step back so that he releases me.

I'm not prepared when the elevator doors finally open. Instead of a hallway with multiple apartments, he ushers me into the large two-story foyer of a penthouse suite.

Holy crap.

"You live here?"

He gives me a cocky-ass grin. "Like it?"

"It's…" My mouth hangs open and I clamp it shut, shaking my head. "It's a little much for one person."

He laughs. "Come on. I'll show you the bedroom."

The bedroom.

This is seriously going to happen.

I follow him down the hall, past the open concept kitchen and living room with floor to ceiling windows. The master bedroom is twice the size of my apartment, the bed the central focus.

He places my bags in the corner of the room and nods at a second door on the far side of the room. "If you want to shower, the bathroom is there."

"Thanks." I swallow past the lump in my throat. The thought of a warm shower is almost overwhelming. It's been weeks since my apartment had hot water.

For a long moment, he stands there watching me, his expression undiscernible. Then he gives a sharp nod and turns to leave the room.

Alone with my thoughts, I start to question everything.

What the hell am I doing here? I should be out looking for Drew, or at least trying to figure out what I'm going to do about Jax.

I can still leave. There's nothing stopping me.

But I don't want to. I feel safe here. Safe with him – *with Henry.*

I shouldn't want this. I'm used to feeling empty, hollow. And I can't explain the overwhelming need for him to fill that void.

One night. I can give myself that. One night of pleasure. One night to feel safe, to feel treasured. I deserve at least that.

I grab my toothbrush from my overnight bag and head to the bathroom. The shower, if you can call it that, looks like something out of a movie, and it takes me a second to figure out how to turn it on. Once I do, I undress quickly, and step under the steaming water, allowing the warmth to ease some of the tension from my body.

My mind drifts to *him,* and a raw ache starts in my center, pulsating between my legs, and my breasts heavy, nipples hard.

I've never lusted over a man. Not like this.

One night, I remind myself. One night to forget the hell that is my life.

I turn the water off and dry myself with a large plush towel. There's a robe, like you see in commercials for fancy hotels, hanging on the back of the door. Biting my lip, I run my fingers over the softness and sigh. I'm sure he wouldn't mind if I borrowed it for the night.

A small moan escapes my lips when I pull it on. I've never been into material things, never had the luxury, but I could get used to the softness that wraps around me.

With a deep breath, I open the door, and have to blink several times for my eyes to adjust to the darkness that greets me.

A shadowy form is sprawled out on the mattress, the bottom half covered by the comforter. In the dim light, I can tell his chest is bare, each chiseled ab clearly defined in the shadows. I can't see his eyes, but I know he's watching me. Waiting.

"Come to bed, Keeley." His voice drips with sex and the words go straight between my legs.

I pad across the floor towards the king-size bed, my heart beating a million times per minutes.

No more hesitation. I want this. I just need to get out of my head and do it.

I pull the blankets back and crawl in beside him.

He doesn't move. Not even when I inch towards him, so close that I can feel the heat radiating off his body.

I don't know what I expect, but his next words shock me to the core. "Get some sleep."

Sleep? Is he kidding?

My body is humming with pent-up sexual energy.

"I thought…" I swallow thickly.

"Go to sleep, Keeley."

What game is he playing?

I start to roll towards the edge of the bed, when his arms wrap around me, pulling me back against his chest, so that my backside is snug against his heavy hard on.

His fingers sneak under my robe, finding my breast. A wave of heat rips through my body as his thumb circles the nub, then pinches it lightly.

I groan, wiggling back against him, and he lets out a deep, guttural moan of his own.

His mouth is by my ear, his breath warm on my cheek.

"You want me?"

"Yes," I whimper.

He lets out a low chuckle and brushes his lips against my neck, making my entire body shiver in anticipation.

"It's late and you've had a shitty day. When I do fuck you, I want you to be completely rested, so I can take my time tasting and devouring every part of you." He pinches my nipple again, this time harder, and I let out a little yelp of pleasure mixed with pain. "Now go to sleep before I forget to be a gentleman."

I want to protest. But I'm also grateful. The moment I close my eyes, I realize how tired I really am.

And it feels good to be held. I don't remember the last time anyone just held me.

One night. I can let my walls down for tonight. Cause God only knows what tomorrow will bring.

47

Chapter 6

Keeley

"What's wrong with Lily, Mama?" I clutch Drew's chubby hand in my own, and stand in the bathroom doorway afraid to look at my baby sister's pale face. Her skin and lips have turned blue, and she isn't crying anymore.

"Go back to bed, Keeley. I'll come for you in a few minutes." Mama's kneeling beside the bathtub, a strange look in her eyes as she rocks Lily in her arms.

Drew is whimpering and I have to shush him, so that Mama doesn't yell at him again. But she doesn't look angry anymore. She seems happy.

But I'm scared and I don't know why.

I take Drew back to the bedroom, and tell him to stay in bed. He puts his thumb in his mouth and nods, but I can tell he's scared too.

The man Mama says is our Daddy came again tonight. But this time there was a lot of yelling. And when he left, Mama cried for a long time.

She cries a lot lately. Ever since Lily was born. I think it's cause the man doesn't come by much anymore.

I sneak out of the room, careful not to make a sound. Mama is in her bedroom now, softly singing as she dresses Lily in her prettiest dress, the white one she wore when we went to the big church and they poured water on her head.

"He'll take me back now. Everything will be all right." Mama is talking to herself, her eyes shiny. "He'll take me back."

I don't want to get in trouble, so I tiptoe back to bed, and put my finger to my lips when Drew starts to cry, holding his arms out to me.

"Everything will be all right," I whisper, repeating her words.

Footsteps echo down the hall, clickity ones, and when Mama comes into our room, she's wearing her fancy shoes, and the dark red dress she wears only for the man.

I close my eyes tight and pretend to be asleep.

The floor creaks and I hear Drew whimper.

"Be a big boy and don't cry. You're going to have a bath and then everything is going to be just fine."

When I open my eyes, Drew is gone. And so is Mama. I'm really scared now. It's dark outside and we already had a bath tonight. I always make sure Drew has his first.

"Key-key." Drew cries for me.

I jump out of bed and run to the bathroom, even though I know Mama is going to be mad.

Her back is to me. "Be a good boy and go to sleep."

He can't sleep in the tub.

I take a step closer.

Drew's face is under the water, eyes big and scared.

"Mama, stop." I pull at her arms, but she doesn't let him go. I hit her, scratch at her face, but she continues to hold him down. "He can't breathe. Mama, please, stop."

I bite down on her arm, and she lets out a cry.

Drew sits up and starts to cough.

Mama grabs at me, but I'm quicker and she slips on the wet floor, hitting her head on the toilet.

I help Drew out of the tub.

"He doesn't want me." There's blood on her head and on her arms where I bit her. She lays on the floor, crying. "Because of you, he doesn't want me anymore."

I cry too. But I know we can't stay.

"Come on." I pull on Drew's wet arm, and run to Mama's room.

Lily is still asleep, lying like a doll on the bed. I'm not allowed to pick her up without Mama, but I don't want to leave her here.

She's heavy, and I struggle to hold her.

My arms feel like they're going to fall off by the time we make it out of the apartment and up the two flights of stairs to Mrs. Hutson's apartment. She's the lady that watches us when the man comes over, and I know she'll help.

I bang on the door, trying to stop the tears from falling down my cheeks. I need to be brave for Drew and Lily.

Mrs. Hutson looks mad when she opens the door. She's wearing her pajamas and her hair is in rollers. Then she looks down at us, and her eyes go wide.

She looks as scared as I feel, which makes me even more afraid. Her fingers shake when she takes Lily from my arms.

The police come. And the people who drive the ambulance. They keep looking at me and Drew with funny faces, and whispering.

They take Lily away. I scream and yell at them that I need to go with her. That she's going to be scared without me.

Mrs. Hutson tries to hold me, but I don't want her to touch me. I just want my sister. And my Mom.

Drew is crying, sitting on the couch, and there's a strange lady with him.

They're going to take him away too.

"No," I scream at the lady. Ready to fight her if I have to. "I won't let you take him."

Drew wraps his arms around my neck, and we sit on the floor, both crying. And I promise him that I'll never let anyone take him away from me. Ever.

Chapter 7

Henry

"Dammit Keeley, wake up." I shake her shoulders, trying desperately to wake her from whatever nightmare she's reliving.

She thrashes against me, her mouth open in a silent gasp as though she's trying to scream. But no sound comes out.

Her eyes open, wide and unseeing. She fights me when I try to hold her, but I don't let go.

"I've got you."

She glances frantically around the room, then at me. I see the moment she remembers where she is, remembers who I am. She goes limp in my arms like all the fight has been ripped from her.

"Henry?" She blinks up at me, the blue of her eyes so vivid it takes my breath away.

"You're all right, sweetheart." I brush her hair off her face. Her forehead is damp with perspiration, cheeks stained with tears.

The utter hopelessness in her gaze breaks something deep in my chest.

I know with every cell in my body that she's the girl from my dreams. The one I swore to defend.

Twenty years ago I gave her something I've never given another woman – my vow. It may have been spoken with a child's voice, but it's the man's heart that will honor it now.

She tries to push away from me, but I tighten my hold.

"I need to find Drew," she whispers, grief thick in her voice.

"We'll find him. I promise."

Slowly, I feel her relax against me.

"It was just a nightmare. I've got you." I hold her face between my hands, stroking her cheeks with the pads of my thumbs.

Her face is clean of makeup, and I see in the earlier morning light how beautiful she really is. Not that fake, made-up beauty, but the real kind. The kind of beauty that can break a man's soul and make him do all kinds of fucked up things.

Shit, I haven't even kissed the woman, but I know I'm in deeper than I ever thought possible. There's nothing I won't do to make her mine. To make sure no one ever hurts her again.

I brush my lips over her forehead, and let out a low, uneven breath.

We lay like that for several minutes, her body molded against mine.

"I'm sorry," she says softly, her small fists clenched against my bare chest. She's still trembling, but it's no longer from fear. I can almost smell her arousal, it's so thick between us. She blinks up at me, blue eyes wanting, needing, and so fucking vulnerable. "I should go."

No chance in hell, sweetheart.

Her robe has come undone, exposing her shoulder and the top of one breast. I trace the outline of the tattoo that runs along her clavicle and across. I noticed it last night, some kind of flower – a lily, I think. I don't usually like tattoos, but on her it's sexy.

I lower my mouth, tasting the skin, running my tongue over the ink.

"Henry?" I hear the mixed emotions in her voice. Fear mixed with want.

"Let me take care of you." My hand slips under the robe, brushing over her breast, the nipple hardening against my touch. I have to stifle the groan that builds in my throat.

Her hands start to go lower, fingers edging under the elastic of my boxer briefs.

I capture her wrists. I know what she intends, but I don't want to rush things. I'm going to take my time. Devour every inch of her body.

Her brows furrow, and her bottom lip sticks out in a small pout.

I chuckle, wrapping her arms around my neck.

"I said I'm going to take care of *you*." I can tell it's not something she's used to. But the primal part of my brain wants nothing more than to consume her, torment her until she surrenders fully, and admits she's mine.

With my knee, I nudge her legs apart, and trail my hand down her hip, pushing the robe back and exposing every delectable inch of her.

"So fucking gorgeous."

For a moment, I'm lost in her beauty and my chest tightens with emotions I've never felt before.

I cup her cheek and run my thumb across her bottom lip. Her mouth parts slightly, her gaze hungry and wanting.

The first touch of our lips and I know I'm a goner.

She arches beneath me, her fingers digging into my shoulder and I taste her moan. That's all I need to lose control. I devour her mouth, pleased when she returns my kiss with equal abandon.

Desire swirls through me like a fucking tornado. My balls ache and my cock is like steel, ready to dive deep and explode within her, and I have to fight the urge to take her swiftly.

She deserves more than just a quick fuck. She deserves to be worshiped, and that's what I intend to do.

I travel down her body, kissing her neck, breasts, stomach, trailing down to the soft curls between her thighs.

Her hands are in my hair, and her eyes are half-lidded and slightly glazed when she looks at me, burning with passion and need.

When I swipe my tongue over her clit she jerks in response, arching upward, seeking more of my mouth. She's so damn responsive.

I slide my tongue inside her and fuck her with short, rapid strokes. The taste of her is pure heaven.

She whimpers and her hands tighten in my hair, pulling me close as I work my tongue over her clit, and my fingers inside her pussy. The sounds she's making are driving me insane.

"Henry." My name is a harsh moan on her lips, sending a thrill down my spine and making my cock jerk in response.

Her muscles tighten around me, and I know she's close, I can feel her body vibrating with the need of her release. I push harder until her body is shuddering beneath me, and she goes over the edge with a cry of pure pleasure.

I can't hold back the groan that rumbles from my chest as she comes against my mouth. I've never tasted anything so sweet.

My self-control is disintegrating. If I don't take her soon, I'm going to fucking explode. No other woman has done this to me, made me feel like this. She's like a drug pouring through my veins, stripping away any willpower I have left.

And I'm going to fuck her until she's mindless with it, until her nightmares and fears are obliterated. Until she has no other option but to admit she's mine.

Chapter 8

Keeley

I fight to simply breathe. Even if I want to, I can't resist his touch. All I can do is melt into him. Enjoy every heated sensation.

I arch toward him, needing more, and a low, muted groan vibrates between my thighs.

"You're killing me." His voice is rough, thick with arousal, his gaze dark, swirling with sexual power and something more. Something possessive.

He crawls up the bed, then reaches over me, opening the drawer of the bedside table and pulling out a condom.

"Don't stop."

"Not even a possibility, sweetheart." His cock springs free as he rolls his briefs down and over his thick, muscular thighs.

I swallow hard at the size of him. When I look up and catch his gaze, his lips twitch up in a smug grin.

He tears open a condom and rolls it over the length of his wide cock. Every muscle in his body seems to tense as he strokes himself, dark eyes never wavering from me. It's the hottest thing I've ever seen. And the need to touch him, to feel him inside of me is overwhelming.

When I reach out to run my hands down his chiseled abs, he catches my wrists and pulls me down, my back against the mattress, one heavy thigh between my legs.

"You have no idea how much I'm going to enjoy being inside of you."

It's been too long since I'd been touched. Too long since I'd felt the hard length of an erection pressed against me, because my senses are on overload, and I can barely form a cohesive thought.

His lips are on mine, and he growls into my mouth, "Do you have any fucking idea how beautiful you are?"

I've been told before, but I've never actually felt it until this moment.

I need this. His touch. His kiss. Or maybe my brain just needs an excuse to take what my body demands.

His thumb strokes across my clit and I swear I can feel the touch in every nerve ending in my body.

It's too much. My heart is racing, my breath coming hard and fast. My body aches for him in ways I never thought possible.

"Please," I cry out, shocked by the desperation in my voice.

"I like when you beg, sweetheart." He positions himself above so that his cock is nudged against my pussy, and I wiggle beneath him desperately. His fingers grip my hips, holding me steady. "But we're going to do this my way. My timing."

A rush of excitement shoots through me. The dominance in his voice, the edge of control and power beneath his dark gaze turns me to putty in his hands.

In this moment, there's no denying that I'm his.

I watch as the swollen head of his cock eases into me. He's huge, and I can feel the stretch of my muscles as I relax to accommodate the width of him.

A small cry tears from my throat as I take more of him. Then, in one hard stroke, he buries himself inside of me.

I gasp, my fingers digging into his arms. He holds himself still inside me, and our gazes lock. If I could stay locked in the moment, I would.

When he starts to move, I'm all but helpless against the pleasure that tears through me. The need for him drowns out the warning that this will only end in heartbreak.

His hands are on me, cupping my ass, molding my breast.

He eases back, and I wrap my legs around his hips, feeling the loss of his hard flesh inside me, and try to pull him back.

"My timing," he chuckles, nipping at my bottom lip, before trailing his lips down my throat. I tremble when he takes my nipple between his teeth, swirling his tongue around the hard bud.

Without warning, he thrusts into me, lodging his cock deeper than before, sending out a flood of sensations racing through my body. He doesn't give me time to adjust before pulling out, then slamming into me again.

His lips cover mine as his hips begin to move fast and steady, and I swear I feel each stroke in the very core of my being. Waves of sensation gather and build, until I'm completely lost in the ecstasy that threatens to consume me.

Nothing exists but the feel of him moving inside of me.

Lust. Hunger. Desire. Whatever it is that drives me, I know that I'll never be the same afterwards.

His kiss becomes more urgent, and I return it, taking his mouth every bit as hard as he takes mine. Our tongues roll and clash, our lips molding against each other.

Heat lashes through me, whipping over my flesh, driving me higher, closer to the point where I feel like my entire body is going to explode with the pleasure of it.

My heavy breaths become moans and I tighten my legs around his thrusting hips, lifting closer to him, trying to catch every last sensation that tears through my body. I clench around his cock and pressure tightens within me, until it's burning out of control and explodes like wildfire across my flesh, through my womb.

The orgasm is so intense, so soul shattering that when I try to scream his name, I only have breath left for a whispered cry.

He thrusts hard, deep, one more time, before his body stiffens and I feel his own release explode within me.

"Fucking hell," he whispers harshly against my ear.

He rolls onto his back, pulling me with him, so that his arms are wrapped around me in an intimate embrace.

At first I freeze, unused to being held.

I lay still, listening to his harsh breathing, unable, or unwilling to move.

We're both silent, which is good, because I don't know if I'd trust my voice to speak. I try to regain some semblance of control over my shattered senses, but he's completely undone me.

I know I should move, before my mind starts to play tricks on me that this is anything more than it is, but I already know it's too late for that.

Where am I supposed to go from here? I know this man will never be mine. But for the briefest moment, he's melted the steel cage I've kept around my heart.

Dangerous. That's what he is.

As if sensing my mood, he places his hand under my chin and forces me to look at him.

"You okay?"

I give a small smile and nod, still not trusting my voice.

"I have to go into the office." He kisses my forehead, then rolls out of bed, a sexy grin on his lips. He discards the condom in the wastebasket beside the bed.

My chest tightens. So this is it. I shouldn't have expected anything more.

Pulling the robe around my shoulders, I throw my legs over the side of the bed.

"I'll get dressed and leave."

I don't hear him move, but the next thing I know, I'm pinned to the bed, his hard body covering mine.

"I didn't ask you to leave," he growls, trailing his lips down my throat.

"I thought–"

"That I was kicking you out?" He looks at me, brows raised, then shakes his head. "I told you, you're staying here. I have a couple meetings this morning, then I'll be back and we can sit down and figure out what we're going to do."

"I don't want you to get involved." My chest tightens at the concern I see in his eyes.

"Too late, sweetheart." He kisses me roughly, then bounds from the bed towards the bathroom. A moment later, I hear the soft hum of the shower.

Something I haven't felt in years stirs inside of me – *hope*.

Chapter 9

Henry

"Asher said you left early last night." My sister, Becca stands in the doorway of my office, brown eyes narrowed on me. She flicks her dark hair over one shoulder and purses her lips.

As usual, she looks like's she's just come off the runway during fashion week. White blouse, navy blue, flared slacks, four-inch Gucci heels. The entire outfit, which I'm assuming she paid for with my credit card, probably cost more than Keeley makes in an entire month working at the club.

Made – I correct myself. She's currently unemployed, which suits me just fine. Having her in my bed twenty-four-seven sounds like fucking heaven. But from what I know about Keeley, she'd never be content just sitting around the apartment all day.

Once this whole Drew thing is handled, I'll make sure to find out what her qualifications are, and find a place for her at Caldwell Industries. There's no way I'm letting her go back to waitressing, because every cell in my body screams in protest at the thought of her being harassed nightly in one of those damn clubs.

"I'm busy, Becca." I scan the file my elderly assistant, Greta, places on my desk in front of me, then scribble my signature at the bottom. "Some of us have to work."

Not one to take a hint, Becca moves into the room and lets out an exaggerated sigh. "Asher thinks you don't like him."

"I don't," I grumble, handing the document back to Greta who tries unsuccessfully to hide a smile. The asshole has always rubbed me the wrong way. That he had my little sister come and petition for him, just makes me hate the fucker more.

"Would you like me to cancel your next appointment?" Greta asks, looking between Becca and me.

"That won't be necessary."

Becca's lips tighten, but she doesn't disagree. "I'll be quick."

As quick as it takes me to write another check. Which is most likely why she's here.

Greta nods, giving me a sympathetic look, before leaving.

"Sit." I lean back in my chair and try my best to hide my frustration. I have a shitload of paperwork to get through before I can get back to Keeley. The last thing I need is to get in another argument with my sister about her weasely little fiancé.

She pouts, but takes a seat in one of the black leather chairs across from me.

"You could at least try. He's really great once you get to know him. I thought we could go out for dinner sometime next week, and–"

I narrow my eyes on her, but instead of continuing her little rant, she shifts uncomfortably under my gaze and fidgets with the clutch she carries.

Shit. She's got that look she gets when she's about to drop a bomb.

"What's wrong?"

"Maybe this isn't a good time," Becca says, a nervous lilt to her voice.

"Spit it out." I tap my fingers on the desk and narrow my eyes, waiting.

"Asher and I were just going through the guest list for the wedding..." She rings her hands together.

The fucking wedding again.

"And?"

She takes a deep breath, then the words tumble from her lips in one big rush, "Asher's family are close friends with the Sullivans, and his parents have asked that they be invited. I told Asher that it wasn't a good idea, but he insisted. I know with your history–"

"No." I love my sister, but there are some things I'm not willing to do...even for her. Facing Abby's parents again is one of them.

"It's my wedding." Becca blinks up at me, her eyes already shimmering with unshed tears.

"And as long as I'm paying for it, they're not coming." It's a low blow. The money is just as much hers as mine. But my father was old-school, and a bit of a prick. He left her share of the money in my name until her thirtieth birthday, or until she married.

It's one of the reasons I'm so against her and Asher. I doubt either of them would be so eager to tie the knot if there weren't a quarter of a billion dollars at stake.

Not that I totally disagree with my father's decision. Becca's always been impulsive. If she'd received the money four years ago when Dad died, I have no doubt she would already burned through it.

"Henry, please. Asher thought–"

"I don't give a shit what Asher thinks." I rub the back of my neck and ignore the pained look she gives me. "They're not coming."

"It was ten years ago. At some point, you need to move on. I know you don't want to tell them the truth, but maybe–"

"They know the truth." I laugh bitterly. "Abby is dead because of me."

"Only *you* believe that."

A low, dark chuckle forms in my throat. "You think I don't know that they blame me? Shit, her father called me a murderer in front of the entire church at the funeral."

"He was grieving."

"Yeah." I drag my fingers through my hair and look away. "And he was right."

"No." She shakes her head, brown eyes full of sympathy. "If they knew what really happened–"

"It wouldn't make a damn difference." I push my chair back and stand, turning my back and glance out the window at the city below.

"If anyone was to blame it was her parents. Or the asshole who–"

"Don't." I turn on her, jaw clenched, every muscle vibrating with tension. Becca's the only person I ever told the truth, and sometimes I regret telling her. Better to have people think I was responsible than to look at me with the pity I see in her eyes now.

"I'm just saying, you weren't the only one who missed the signs."

I know she's right, but they weren't the ones that found her. They didn't get the panicked call that night saying she couldn't take it anymore. She practically told me she was going to take her life. I should have gone to her right away. Not waited, because I was fucking some girl, whose name I can't even remember.

If I'd gone when she'd called, I could have stopped her. She'd be alive. Probably married with children by now. Not buried ten feet in the ground, rotting, her ghost haunting my dreams every night.

Sure, the Sullivans were shitty parents. I get that it isn't every parents' wildest dream for their eighteen-year-old to come home knocked up, but they practically disowned her when they found out. Told her to get an abortion or they'd dissolve her trust fund. *Fucking assholes.*

They assumed the baby was mine. The fucked up thing is that other than in the second grade behind the portables at school, we never even kissed.

But Abby was terrified to tell them who the real father was. Some low-end asshole from the wrong side of the tracks. She loved the guy, gave him her virginity, and in exchange he gave her an ectopic pregnancy and an STD.

Her parents still don't know the truth. I never told them and I never will. Not for their sake, but for Abby's memory. What the hell do I care if they think I'm the asshole who destroyed their daughter's life? *Because in my own way I was.*

But Becca's right. It's been ten fucking years. If the Sullivans want to come to the damn wedding, who the hell am I to say no.

"I'll tell Asher to take them off the list." Becca mumbles behind me.

"No." I pinch the bridge of my nose and let out a slow, uneven breath. "Let them come."

Becca's eyes widen, then she gives me a small smile. "Thank you."

I give a sharp nod, grateful when the phone rings. Michael Harrison's name displays on the screen.

"I need to take this."

Having got what she wanted, Becca turns to leave, but not without adding, "Let's do dinner next week. Tuesday. Just you, me and Asher."

Swallowing a cynical retort, I ignore her and answer the call.

"Hey, boss." Michael's gruff voice growls out on the other end. "Stewie said you've got some work for me."

An ex-marine and retired cop, the man has been in charge of my security team for the past five years. He's also my closest confidant. There's no one I trust more, which is why I'm assigning him to finding Keeley's brother. He knows how to dig up dirt and how to bury it, which I'm assuming is going to come in handy in this case.

"I need you to look into someone for me." I pull out the plastic driver's license that I took from Keeley's wallet, flipping it over in my fingers. It was an asshole thing to do without her permission, but I need to know what I'm up against if I'm going to help her.

I scan the license and send it to him.

"How deep do you want me to look?"

"I want everything." Because if she is who I think, then I've got a hell of a lot more to worry about than just her brother.

"Pretty girl." Michael chuckles on the other end.

Pretty doesn't even begin to describe her. She's fucking gorgeous.

"Yeah," I mumble, an edge of possessiveness to my voice that I can't hide. "She's got a brother. Drew or Andrew. The kid's in trouble. I want him found as quickly as possible."

Michael grunts. "What kinda shit we talking about?"

"Drugs. Theft. Possibly gang related."

There's silence on the other end, followed by a low whistle. "All right, boss."

"I want you to run a background check on John Sullivan as well. I have a feeling he's connected to her and the kid in some way." It's a big assumption based on a twenty-year-old memory.

Michael lets out a heavy breath.

"One more thing." I pick up the driver's license and rub my thumb over Keeley's picture. "She'll be staying with me for a bit. I'm going to need some extra security around the place. I want someone watching who comes in and who goes out at all times."

"I'll send Ty and Lance over right away."

"Tell them to stay covert. I don't want to scare her."

"Sure thing, boss." I can hear the concern in his voice and I know he wants more information than I've given him.

But in all fucking honesty, I'm still trying to process everything that's happened myself.

All I know is that the woman is mine, and I'm going do everything in my power to protect her.

Chapter 10

Keeley

I snuggle into the soft mattress and smile when I feel Henry's arms wrap around me. What should have been a one-night-stand has turned into a one-week luxury vacation with Mr. Tall, Dark, and Sinfully Perfect starring as my own personal sex god.

When he moves closer, spooning me, I can feel his erection against my ass. His hands roam down my body, over my hips, my leg, then back up, cupping my breast, and teasing the nipple.

I let out a small moan and wiggle against him, desperate to be closer.

He murmurs in my ear, "I could get used to this."

So could I. That's what I'm afraid of. Despite how amazing he's been, I know this can't last. I still haven't found or heard from Drew, and despite Henry's insistence that I let him worry about it, I can't shake the feeling that I should be doing something more.

I roll onto my back, and Henry takes advantage of my new position by moving between my thighs. His dark hair hangs in mussed waves over his forehead and he smiles down at me like I'm the most beautiful thing he's ever seen.

"God, you're gorgeous," he says. Even though he doesn't say it, his expression says he owns me, that I'm his. *And I know it's true.*

Soft orange and gold light drifts through the window, from the morning sun as it peeks through the open blinds, reflecting in the soft brown hue of his eyes.

I reach up and run my hand against the dark scruff on his jaw.

He captures my hand and kisses my palm. A powerful, electric sensation travels down my arm, warming my entire body. I can't even begin to understand the chemistry between us. It's so natural, and yet primal and possessive at the same time.

In the back of my mind, I know I shouldn't still be here. I should have left before my emotions started to get involved. But for the first time in my life, I actually feel safe – cherished.

"What are you thinking about?" His brows draw down in concern as if sensing my mood. It's sometimes overwhelming how intuitive he is. Like he can read my thoughts.

"Nothing." I wrap my arms around his neck, not wanting to wreck the moment. "Just how good you feel."

I pull his lips back down to mine and he groans into my mouth. Heat ricochets through my body, and every nerve ending seems to fire at the same time. I've never wanted or lusted after a man like this, and it's terrifying. Even more scary are the feelings that stir in my chest when I look at him.

Love. Lust. The lines between the two are blurred. I just know that in a perfect world, I'd never leave his arms.

His cock nudges at my entrance, ready and waiting, and I fight the urge to pull him into me, to let him take me with nothing between us.

Get yourself together, Keeley. The last thing I need is to get knocked up. Hell, I can barely take care of myself. What would I do with a baby?

"Condom," I say breathlessly against his lips.

He reaches past me, grabbing a condom from his quickly depleting stash, then rolls it over the long length of his erection.

I cling to him, my entire body clamping around him as he buries himself fully inside me.

He surrounds me. Touches me. Fills me. There isn't a part of our bodies that don't touch. He's locked inside of me, tight and hot, and I know there's nothing better in the world then this feeling.

His hands are on me, exploring my body with deft fingers, roaming down my hips, cupping my ass, pulling me tight against his chiseled body. His thumb slides over my sensitive nipple, and my back arches. He groans before his mouth finds mine as he pulls back, then slams into me again.

We lock gazes, and I hold on tight, never wanting to let go.

"God, you completely undo me," he rasps, resting his forehead against mine as he pushes into me so deep that I all I can do is gasp.

He takes me hard and fast, and it isn't long before we're both crying out in pleasure, and the world around me blurs.

Pure heaven. If I only I could live in this moment, where nothing can touch me, where everything seems right, and only he matters.

"So fucking good," he whispers against my neck when the tremors of our orgasms finally cease. He pushes up on his forearms and glances down at me, then places a kiss on the tip of my nose. "Yeah, I could definitely wake up to this every morning."

I smile weakly and nod.

"No more nightmares?" His thumb brushes over my cheek, and he kisses me one more time before he pulls out of me.

I shake my head, but it's a lie. My dreams are haunted by images of Drew lying cold and lifeless in a gutter somewhere, or by Lily's soft cries, my mom's tormented screams.

He gives a small frown, then sits up and discards the condom. When he looks back at me, his expression is clouded.

"You know if you want to talk about anything, I'll listen." He traces the curve of my jaw, and waits for me to respond.

I know he wants me to talk about my past, but I'm not ready. I don't know if I'll ever be ready. Some things are just too painful to talk about.

Instinctively, I touch the tattoo on my shoulder. I got it a few years ago, on the anniversary of Lily's death. Drew was angry with me. He hates any reminders of her – of our mom. He has enough anger for both of us, even though I don't think he really remembers much of what happened.

"I have to go into the office today. I thought if you're interested you might want to meet Becca and go shopping."

"Your sister?" I sit up, pulling the covers over my chest, and lean against the headboard.

"She wants to meet you, and it would be good for you to get out of the apartment." He stands and stretches, displaying all his male-perfectness, then moves into the large walk-in closet. When he returns he's wearing a pair of dark gray slacks, and a white button-down that hangs open displaying his chiseled abs. "Plus, you're going to need a dress for the wedding, and–"

"Wedding?" He's told me all about his younger sister and the guy she's marrying, but I never expected to be invited to the ceremony. The thought makes my stomach twist.

"It's next Saturday. I told you that."

"I know. I just didn't think…" I shake my head and chew on my bottom lip.

He sits on the edge of the bed, puts his palms beside my hips, and leans towards me. "It would mean a lot to me if you went."

"Okay," I say, despite the trepidation I feel.

He kisses me roughly, then pulls back. "Good. I'll tell Becca to pick you up at noon. She'll help you find a suitable dress."

"I don't have…" I grab his hand when he starts to stand and the corners of his lips drop. "I mean…I can't afford anything fancy."

My cheeks warm in embarrassment.

"Becca has my credit card. I want you to buy whatever you want. You don't need to worry about money. Not anymore."

He cups my chin when I look down at my hands. I can't take money from him. It isn't right.

"I'm not going to be a charity case."

"That's not what I was implying." He narrows his eyes, and there's a hint of anger there. "You're my…" He rubs his hands through his hair and shakes his head. "Think of it as a gift."

Shit. I don't want to fight. But it needs to be said.

"This whole week has been like a dream. But–"

"But what?"

"Once this ends, then what am I left with? No job. No apartment. I need to start thinking about my future."

"Your future is here." He takes my hand and places it over his heart, and I can feel the soft thumping rhythm beneath my palm.

I wish I could believe him. I want to believe him. But one day he'll get tired of me, and then what? I'll be out on the streets, heartbroken. Just like my mom when my father decided she was nothing but an inconvenience.

I won't let myself be that woman.

"Keeley?" Henry is frowning at me, eyes full of concern. "I'll never leave you with nothing."

The sincerity in his voice makes my heart race. It's not that I don't believe him. I just can't put my faith, my future in one person's hands. It's too dangerous.

"I don't need you to take care of me." I pull my hand back and he sighs.

"I wish I could stay and discuss this further," he says, standing and buttoning his shirt. "But I have an eight-thirty meeting." He leans over and kisses the top of my head. "We'll talk more tonight."

He grabs his wallet and keys, before he heads out of the room.

As I watch him go, I feel a lump forming in my throat. No idea where I'm supposed to go from here.

Chapter 11

Keeley

By the time noon rolls around my nerves are shot. I should never have agreed to go shopping with Becca. I'm not good with strangers, and from everything Henry's told me about her, I expect a self-absorbed, prima donna with too much money and time on her hands. I'm not prepared for the energetic, young woman who practically bounces into the apartment and wraps her arms around me in a tight hug.

"I'm so excited to meet you," she says, nearly squeezing the oxygen from my lungs.

She pulls back and her wide smile dims suddenly. She seems almost upset by my appearance. And compared to her fancy clothes and hair, I don't blame her.

Self-conscious, I take a small step back and wrap my arms around my chest.

"Sorry. I don't mean to stare." She's still frowning, but I can see there's nothing malicious in her gaze. "It's just." She tilts her head as if she's studying me. "You just look a lot like someone I used to know."

"Oh," I say, not knowing how else to respond. "Henry said the same thing when he first met me."

"I imagine he did," she says cryptically. Then her face brightens again, and she takes my hand. "I can't wait to hear about everything. It's just so exciting."

"Everything?"

"Yes, everything." She waves her arms in the air. "I want to know how you and Henry met. How long you've been dating. How long it took him to ask you to move in."

"He didn't tell you?"

"Henry doesn't tell me anything. That's why I'm so excited to finally meet you." She glances down at my clothes, then does a small circle around me like she's appraising me "I love this look you've got going on. It's like bohemian mixed with the girl next door. Super fun."

"Bohemian?" I glance down at my worn in jeans and oversized blouse that I bought at the thrift shop last month.

"You're funny." She laughs, linking her arm with mine and practically dragging me towards the elevator. "So in all seriousness, how did you manage to get my brother to settle down?"

"He's not…I mean, we're not that serious."

"Serious enough to move in together." She winks, stepping into the elevator when it opens.

I shrug, not knowing how much I should tell her. What can I say? The truth is I don't really know how to process the bombardment of emotions that Henry evokes. All I know is that he somehow fills the places in my heart that have been long left empty and aching.

79

Becca must sense my reluctance to share because she changes the subject quickly.

"So what stores do you like to shop at? I prefer Louis Vuitton, Prada, Gucci. But if there's somewhere else you'd like to go let me know."

I don't know much about any of those stores, but they all sound expensive.

Becca talks non-stop all the way to the car that's parked outside of the apartment, and it doesn't take me long to realize that she idolizes her brother.

After only twenty minutes, I know every trivial detail about her wedding, her bridesmaids, and the man she's about to marry. While there is genuine affection in her voice for Asher, I also note that she's worried about the disconnect between him and Henry.

"I just wish Henry would give Asher a chance. He can be so black and white sometimes, but I'm sure you already know that." She sighs and picks up a pink sequenced dress that the sales associates picked up, and curls her lip. "This is a definite no."

We go to three different stores and try on numerous dresses before Becca is finally satisfied with one.

"I can't buy this," I say, staring incredulously at the four-digit price tag of the dress I have on. A soft blue silk that drapes around my breasts and hips, and dipping seductively low at the back.

I wonder if she realizes that there are people in the world who don't walk around with an inexhaustible supply of credit.

"But Henry will love it on you," she squeals, clapping her hands. "It matches your eyes perfectly. With your hair up, it'll be absolutely stunning."

I glance at my reflection and can't help the small smile that curves my lips. Becca is right, the dress is beautiful. But it's worth more than I normally make in an entire month.

"Maybe something a little less expensive."

Becca shakes her head, and I realize I'm about to experience the stubborn streak Henry warned me about.

"No. You're getting this one. I insist."

"But—"

"No buts." She turns to the woman who was helping us and gives her a set of instructions to have the dress shipped to Henry's apartment. When she turns back to me, she looks almost as giddy as if she had bought it for herself. "Now hurry up and get dressed. I'm starving and there's this cute little sushi restaurant that just opened around the corner."

It's hard not to like the woman, but by the end of our shopping and lunch date, I'm exhausted.

"This was so much fun," Becca says, hugging me for what has to be the hundredth time today. "I can't wait to do it again. I've been trying to get Henry to join Asher and me for dinner, maybe you can convince him. It'll be great. Just the four of us. Sometime next week?"

The way she looks at me, I can't do anything but nod and say I'll try.

Her face flushes with happiness that's almost contagious, and I realize I'm smiling when the car rolls away into traffic.

Walking towards the entrance of Henry's building, I feel a sudden heaviness, like someone is watching me. I freeze and look over my shoulder. But there's nothing out of the ordinary. Just regular people going about their business.

Still, my heart pounds violently against my ribcage and a fresh rush of adrenaline races through my veins.

Jax. I don't see him, but I swear I can feel him, hidden in the shadows, waiting, watching.

Maybe I'm just being paranoid, but I don't take any chances. I quicken my pace, rushing through the large glass doors. I don't think I take a full breath until I'm safely back in Henry's penthouse.

Coward, my brain rebukes.

I stretch out my fingers and try to make them stop shaking.

"I can't keep doing this," I mumble, sitting down heavily on the couch and pulling the throw over my shoulders. I can't keep hiding, waiting for Jax to strike. Waiting for Drew to finally tell me where the hell he is. Waiting for Henry to finally realize that I'm more trouble than I'm worth.

I glance around at the ridiculously large apartment, with the marble floors and fancy furniture and know that I don't belong here. But I know if I leave, if I run from Henry, that I'll regret it my entire life.

I shake my head, knowing I need to make a choice, and soon. Because the longer I stay here, the harder it'll be when this whole fairytale comes crashing down around me.

Chapter 12

Keeley

Henry saunters into the kitchen, dropping his keys and briefcase on the counter.

All I can think is, God, he's gorgeous. His dark hair is mussed, like he's been running his fingers through it. The top buttons of his shirt have been undone, and his tie loosened. His sleeves are rolled carelessly over his muscular forearms, the white fabric contrasting against his tanned skin.

My first instinct is to wrap my arms around his neck and kiss him. And I can see in the heat of his expression is that he must be thinking something similar.

He moves towards me and reaches out and caresses my cheek, then leans in and presses his lips softly against mine. His fingers grip my chin, and when he pulls back slightly, his gaze all but consumes me.

A tingling feeling starts at the base of my skull and travels down my spine.

"You take my breath away every time I see you." The rasp of his voice sends a rush of sensations through my body and my cheeks warm.

I've never had someone speak to me the way he does, like I'm actually worth something. And the way he touches me, it's like he's been doing it forever. Like I mean something to him.

Dangerous thoughts, I remind myself. But despite my mind's warnings, I can't help but be transfixed in the moment. To be carried away by the feel of his body against mine. The man's too sexy for *my* own good.

I find myself leaning into him, then his lips are on mine again, and all tenderness is gone, replaced by something almost primal. His hands are on my waist, pulling me closer, and I can't help the soft hum that vibrates on my lips as his mouth all but consumes me.

His kiss is fierce. Possessive.

He pulls back and grins down at me. "I ordered Chinese. It should be here soon."

"Chinese?"

"Unless you prefer to go out for dinner."

I shake my head, frowning. "Chinese is fine."

"How was shopping?"

"It was fun. Becca's great. She really loves you."

He makes a noise in the back of his throat. "Did you find a dress?"

"Yes. They're delivering it here."

"Good."

I nod, and chew on my bottom lip, mind drifting to earlier. I still can't shake the feeling that someone was watching me earlier.

"What's wrong?" His eyes narrow, and he runs his thumb over my bottom lip.

My knees all but give out on me from his touch. My brain is complete mush around him.

"I need to look for Drew." I've already wasted too much time.

I shake my head and turn away from him. What was I thinking staying here?

His arms are around me before I'm able to take another step away, crushing me against his chest, and he glances down at me.

He cups my chin, forcing me to look at him. "I told you I'd help you find your brother and I never break my promise. I have my men looking into it. Michael is going to come by later this evening. He's one of the best P.I.s in the state. Wherever Drew is, he'll find him."

Private investigator? Panic claws at my throat. The last thing Drew or I need is someone looking into our past. If he ever uncovered who our father is, this thing with Jax would seem like a small inconvenience in comparison. He's already made it painfully clear that he wants nothing to do with us, and the threat real if we ever tried to expose him.

"I don't know if that's a good idea."

He captures my chin between his fingers, then leans down and kisses me.

"I'm going to have a shower, then we'll talk." There's a wicked glint in his eyes when he looks down at me. "Unless you'd like to join me."

My entire body screams – *yes*. But I shake my head, needing a moment to cool off and try to gather my thoughts.

Whatever it is I'm doing here, I know it can't last. I should have left when I had the chance, not stuck around and waited like some pathetic teenager with her first crush. There are a million different reasons to leave, and only one to stay – *Him.*

It's not a good enough reason.

But the minute I close my eyes it's his face I see. His full, sensual lips taking mine. The way his large hands feel as they roam over my body. The heaviness of him between my legs, moving inside me.

I shouldn't want him the way I do. I should be out on the streets searching for Drew. God only knows where he is or what's happened to him. He's still not answering my texts, and every time I try to call him his phone goes to voicemail after one ring.

"Don't worry." Henry squeezes my shoulder. "Trust me. I'll do everything I can to help you."

I give him a weak smile.

"You sure you don't want to change your mind and join me in the shower?"

A tempting as it is, I shake my head. "I'll pass."

The frown line between his brow creases, but he doesn't argue.

"Why don't you open a bottle of wine." He kisses my forehead. "Try to relax. I'll just be a few minutes."

When he disappears down the hall, I slump against the counter and rub my eyes. *Wine.* I don't drink much, but right now I could handle a couple glasses. Anything to take the edge off.

There's a bottle of white chilling in the fridge. I scan the label, knowing that it probably cost more than half a month's rent.

I sigh and place it on the counter, then start opening drawers to find a corkscrew. There are so many cabinets and drawers in this damn kitchen, it's almost impossible to find anything. The third drawer I open is filled with what looks like documents, I'm about to close it when my gaze falls on a manila envelope with the name Abby, handwritten in black ink.

It's none of my business what's inside the envelope, but curiosity wins, and I pull the envelope from the drawer. With a heaviness in my chest that warns me I'm about to open Pandora's box, I reach in and pull out the stack of old photos inside.

My breath catches in my throat as I quickly finger through the pile.

The first picture is of a beautiful blonde, blue eyes wide and innocent, her arms wrapped around a younger Henry. They're no older than seventeen or eighteen, but it's clear by the intimate way they hold each other that they're extremely close.

Picture after picture of the two of them together in different locations, on the beach, rock climbing, playing golf. It's clear whoever this Abby is, that Henry was, or is in love with her.

It shouldn't bother me, but it does. I can't help the jealousy that slowly creeps into my chest, tightening my throat.

The girl is beautiful. And the closer I look, the more familiar she seems. But I know I've never met her.

My cell vibrates in my back pocket and I nearly drop the photos. I stuff them back in the envelope and shut the drawer. My fingers shake when I pull out my phone and read the text message on the screen.

I know where your brother is.
My place. 2:30.
Don't even think about trying to fuck with me.

There's no display name, but I know the number. *Jax.*

A chill runs down my spine. If he knows where Drew is then my brother is in real danger.

I glance over my shoulder, down the hall toward the master bedroom. I can still hear the faint hum of the shower.

What do I do?

I know that if I tell Henry about the text, he'll either try to stop me from going, try to go with me, or call the cops – which is *not* going to happen.

God, I was selfish and stupid to think coming here was a good idea. I don't even want to think about what would happen if Jax knew that I went home with Henry after what happened at the club.

I tap my phone against my forehead and curse under my breath. This is my problem, and I have to deal with it myself.

Jax is an asshole. But he's the asshole who holds my brother's life in his hands.

That I'm even second guessing choosing a one-night-stand over my brother Drew makes me sick with guilt.

I take a deep breath and type in a quick response.

I'll be there.

I don't trust Jax. But one thing he isn't is a liar. If he says he knows where Drew is, then he does.

Without another thought, I pull out a pen and paper from one of the drawers and scribble a short note.

Best for both of us that we end it here.
It was fun.
Keeley

I rush to the bedroom to gather my things, hesitating briefly when I hear the shower turn off.

One-night-stand, I remind myself. That's all he is. All he'll ever be. It may have lasted more than one night, but it's still all that it is. All that it was. I know I'm lying to myself even as I think it, but I can't believe in anything else, not if I'm going to be able to walk away.

Steeling my spine, I close my eyes and breathe through the realization that I'm alone and always will be.

I sling my bag over my shoulder and feel something sharp dig into my side. Reaching in, I pull out my old wooden sword and frown. I'm not sure how it even got in there, I know I didn't pack it. Henry seemed oddly fascinated with it, maybe he put it in my bag. *Odd.*

I frown down at it, some faint memory pulling at the back of my mind.

For years, I slept with the sword under my pillow, dreaming of the dark-haired boy who gave it to me. The memory of that day is all but faded, and I'm not sure how much of it is true versus a child's imagination.

Knights and vows.

Dragons and princesses.

The belief that bad guys could be defeated, and happily-ever-after did exist.

Not in my world.

A sad laugh bubbles up from my chest as I move quickly down the hall.

I don't know why I do it, but I place the sword beside my note.

Despite the ache in my chest that wants to believe otherwise, girls like me don't get the fairytale endings. There's no Prince Charming. No dragons. And no white knight to save me. No one is coming to *my* rescue – If I want to survive, I need to be my own hero.

Chapter 13

Henry

I know something is wrong the second I walk out of the bathroom. The apartment is eerily silent, and the warmth I felt a few minutes before is gone.

"Keeley?" I call out, wrapping a towel around my waist.

No answer.

She's gone. I know it even before I find the sword and the scribbled note she left on the kitchen counter. White-hot anger whips up my spine when I read it.

It was fun.

What the fuck?

I start to pace, balling the note in my fist and whipping it across the room.

Something is wrong. It doesn't make sense that she'd run. I know she felt something between us.

But I also have no doubt that she's running *to* someone and I have a bad feeling I know who.

I find my cell and dial Michael.

"I've got men trailing her," he says gruffly before I can speak.

"Good." Thank fucking God I put watchers on the place.

"You want me to bring her back?"

I rub the back of my neck and breathe out heavily. She isn't my fucking prisoner, and I know she'd be pissed if she knew I had someone tagging her, but I can't just let her walk away. Not when her life could be in danger, and not when I still haven't figured out the insane rollercoaster of emotions that I feel for her.

"Just follow her. I want to know *who* she's running to."

I hang up and curl my hands into fists, tempted to punch a hole in the wall.

Her words echo in my head…*Best for both of us that we end it here.*

"No chance in hell, sweetheart."

Because whatever this is between us has only just begun. And I have no intentions of it ending anytime soon.

Chapter 14

Keeley

A heaviness settles over me as I race across the intersection towards the west end. I don't have enough for bus fare, so I have to walk the thirty-six blocks it takes me to get to Gray Street. I know how many blocks there are because I count each one. Anything to take my mind off of what I'm about to do.

What am I about to do? I don't have a plan. Nothing. I know it's not smart, but I'm willing to pay the price if it means keeping Drew safe.

A shiver runs down my spine as a burst of cold air wraps around me, and under the thin material of my shirt. I rub my arms and tuck my chin, pushing my way through the crowded streets.

Maybe when this is all over, I'll finally convince Drew to get the help he needs. I don't know how I'll come up with the money to get him into a good rehab, but somehow I'll figure it out. All I know is I won't give up on him. Ever. Everyone else may have turned their backs on him, on me, but I made a promise that I never would.

I'll get my brother back, and everything will be fine. At least as fine as things can be.

The backfire of an engine a few feet away makes me jump, and I nearly knock over an elderly man walking in the opposite direction.

"I'm so sorry." I help right him, then increase my pace. I need to get this over with before I change my mind and back down.

I can't shake the feeling that I'm being followed, but every time I turn around there's nobody there.

In front of Jax's apartment, I stop and inhale a long, slow breath.

I can do this. I have to do this.

My feet feel like they're filled with cement as I trudge up the two flights of stairs.

Brown stains on the dingy old carpet, water marks on the walls, the smell of multiple spices mixed with a scent of marijuana and body odor – this is the world I'm used to.

Poverty. Alcohol. Drugs. A spiraling pit of doom that once you're sucked into, is nearly impossible to get out of. But somehow I'll get Drew out of it, no matter the sacrifice.

I knock once.

"What?" Comes the dark rasp on the other side.

"It's me," I say, weakly, then straighten my shoulders and clench my jaw, hoping to gain some semblance of strength.

A series of locks and chains click on the other side, then the door opens and Jax stares down at me with cold, dark eyes.

I want to blame him for everything, but in the back of my mind I know he's as much a product of the system as Drew and I. Ten years jumping between foster homes messes with your head in ways *regular* people can never understand. That's not even taking into account what put you in the system to begin with. If you're one of the lucky ones, you come out just slightly broken. For the rest of us, we fight our demons on a daily basis – *and sometimes, like for Drew and Jax, the demons win.*

"You alone?" Jax's nostrils flare as he looks over my shoulder and down the hall.

I nod.

"Smart girl." His lips twist in a smirk, and he opens the door wider. "Come in."

His left eye is swollen and his upper lip is cut from where Henry hit him. The thought of Henry makes me question the sanity of me being here. Maybe I should have told him. But then what?

If I called the cops, Jax would just have one of his goons collect payment, which would most likely be my or Drew's head. Maybe both. If Henry came down here slugging, which I have no doubt he'd do, I'd never get the information I need.

No. This is my only option.

"Where is he?" I try to keep my voice steady, but even I can hear the quiver in it.

Jax's eyes narrow and he motions towards an old, brown leather La-Z-Boy. "Take a seat."

"I'll stand."

"It wasn't a request," he growls.

I cross my arms and lean against the wall knowing if I show even the slightest bit of fear, he'll be all over me.

"I didn't come here for a social visit. I want to know where my brother is."

The old couch creaks when he sits on it, leaning back with one arm slung over the top.

"You're forgetting the little prick stole from me. I want what I'm owed."

"I don't have that kind of money. You already took everything I have when you raided my apartment."

"I never touched your place." His expression never wavers.

"Then who did?" I know the answer even before the words are out of my mouth, but I don't want to believe it.

"Looks like your brother fucked us both over."

I shake my head, my stomach sinking. "He wouldn't."

Jax laughs darkly. "You have no idea what he's capable of."

I shake my head, my breathing quickening. He doesn't know Drew. Not like I do. He's good. He'd never hurt me. Not intentionally.

"Tell me where he is and I'll get your money back. Just promise me you won't hurt him."

He gives a hard mocking laugh, then leans over the glass table and snorts a line of white powder.

"I'm the least of his problems. Or yours." He rubs his nose and makes an awful sound in the back of his throat. "The kid's been racking up debt for the past year."

He sits back, watching me with an antagonizing smirk.

"You lent him money?"

"I'm not that stupid, princess." He laughs arrogantly.

"Then who?" A sinking feeling settles in the pit of my stomach.

"Now that's a good question." He leans over the table again, snorting another line. His eyes are glazed when he glances back at me. "Let's just say your brother has been playing a dangerous game of chance between two very influential drug cartels."

"How mu-much does he owe?" I stumble over the words.

"Word is he managed to rack up almost a hundred grand before someone realized he was manipulating the numbers. I give the little shit some credit though, he's got balls. But once those guys realize he's skipped town, who do you think they'll be coming after?"

My brain can't even process that kind of money. It'd take me a lifetime to pay that much back. But why would Jax lie?

A shiver runs down my spine. "Why are you telling me this?"

He stands and slowly makes his way towards me. Every muscle in my body tenses. I know the look in his eyes. What he's really after. *Me.*

"I don't want to see you hurt." He reaches out and runs a calloused hand over my face. "I can protect you."

"I didn't do anything. They're after Drew, not me."

"They want their money, and they'll get it any way they can. Even if it means digging into Daddy's deep pockets."

I feel the blood drain from my face and my hands go clammy.

"My father's dead."

He chuckles. "Don't play games with me, princess. We both know that's not true. How do you think the little shit gained the cartel's trust? He was using Daddy's name as leverage."

Damn it, Drew. I want to deny the accusation, but it makes sense.

Two years ago, Drew went searching for records of who our father was. Somehow he managed to track down old financial deposits that led back to John Sullivan. When he questioned me about it, I broke down and told him the truth.

It was right after that he started to spiral out of control.

My mother never put John's name on our birth certificates, but I unlike Drew, I was old enough to remember him.

I don't know what Drew thought. That maybe the man would actually want us, that he'd finally claim us as his own. But I knew better, and I tried to warn Drew that contacting him would only end badly.

It had.

I don't know exactly what happened, Drew never told me, but Drew was never the same after. Another reason why I hate John Sullivan with every fiber of my being.

"The man's a sperm donor, nothing more," I hiss.

"Maybe." Jax's fingers snakes behind my neck and tighten in the hair at the nape of my neck.

"He's done everything in his power to make sure no one knows about us. You're insane if you think he'll pay a penny."

"For your sake you better hope that's not true." He leans into me, inhaling a deep breath, then releases me suddenly. "I've done some digging of my own."

I shudder involuntarily when he turns away and moves to the table that's pushed against the far corner of the room. He flips through some papers on the table, pulling out what looks like a cut out of an old obituary.

"I don't know why I didn't put the pieces together before now. The family resemblance is uncanny."

He hands me the clipping and I recognize the photo immediately. I was staring at the exact same picture less than an hour ago in Henry's kitchen. *Abby.*

My breath catches in my throat when I read her name and realize the significance of what Jax is showing me.

Abigail Sullivan.

Daughter of John and Sarah Sullivan.

"A bottle of bleach and the two of you could almost pass as twins." Jax laughs, and runs a hand roughly over my hair.

The more I look at the picture, I know he's right. There's no doubt she's my sister. It's the reason she looked so familiar. She looks like me. I don't know why I didn't see it before. Maybe because I was too wrapped up in jealousy over her relationship with Henry.

My mind is a clusterfuck of thoughts and emotions.

"Why are you showing me this?"

"Think about it, darling. He might be able to deny Drew's claim that he's the sperm donor, but one look at you and nobody will question your paternity. He'll have no choice but to pay whatever amount I ask."

I jerk my head up, finally realizing what he intends. "You plan on ransoming me?"

My heart feels like it's trying to leap out of my throat. This can't be happening.

"We work together and I'll give you your share." He places a hand on the wall beside my head and leans in. "Isn't that what you want, money? To protect little Drew. Or is it revenge?"

"I don't want either."

"Bullshit. And trust me princess, if you don't now, you will."

"I need to go." Panic claws at my throat. My brain is in information overload and I need to get away.

"And run back to Caldwell? I don't think so, princess."

I swallow hard. "You had me followed?"

"I need to keep an eye on my investments." His knuckles brush down my arm making the hairs on the back of my neck stand on end.

"I'll be honest. I was a bit shocked by your choice. But then it hit me. Caldwell. Abby. It all makes sense."

"What are you talking about?"

"I didn't recognize him at first."

"Henry doesn't have anything to do with this."

"Oh, but he does." Jax laughs. "You think that Henry Caldwell would be with someone like you if it wasn't for some gain? Sure, you're a good fuck, but there's never been much in that pretty little head of yours."

"Screw you," I bite out, regretting the words as soon as they pass my lips.

"I have every intention, princess." His eyes glitter with the threat.

I jerk my arm away, but he captures my wrist and sneers.

"The man fucked your sister."

I freeze, the lingering fear in the back of my mind, finally verbalized.

Jax smiles as if reading my thoughts.

"He got her pregnant." He leans in, his voice low as if he's telling me some great secret. I want to close my ears and un-hear it all. "Worse. She killed herself because he wouldn't step up and be the Daddy."

"No."

He smirks. "Don't believe me? Ask him."

I've heard people say time stood still, but I've never experienced it until this moment.

A lump forms in my throat and I can barely swallow past it.

"You're lying."

"Shit. Sometimes I forget how fucking naive you really are."

I glance towards the door. It's my first mistake.

He growls low in his throat and grabs my arm, twisting it behind my back, his other hand goes to my throat, fingers clamping in tight enough to make it difficult to breathe.

"You think you can walk away from this? From me?" His body pushes against me and I can feel his erection against my leg. He lets go of my arm and starts to unbuckle his belt. "I own you now."

"No," I gasp, clawing at his fingers and trying to push him off – my second mistake. He enjoys the fight, and I know it'll only make my punishment worse.

The pressure around my throat increases. I open my mouth to scream, but no sound comes out.

"You'll thank me for this later." His hot, damp breath burns my eyes and I blink back tears.

"You're…insane," I gasp. White pin-pricks of light dance in my vision.

"You can fight me all you want, princess." His fingers tangle in my hair, yanking my head back, his other hand still tight around my throat. "But you'll pay back every dime your brother owes me, plus interest."

He won't kill me. But I know whatever he has planned will be much worse than death.

With every ounce of strength I have left, I bring my knee up hard between his legs. He lets out a howl of pain, and his grip loosens just enough that I'm able to stumble towards the door.

"Ungrateful bitch."

I'm thrown against the wall, his thick hands once again wrapped around my throat, this time in a death grip.

Then the world seems to explode. The door crashes open and two men with guns burst into the room.

Jax's grip unlocks from my throat, but my legs have gone numb, and without him holding me up, I collapse to the floor.

Angry voices scream in my ear, and I'm only faintly aware of the fighting going on around me. Jax doesn't back down, even when the older of the two men shove the barrel of the gun against his forehead.

"Stay down, asshole."

"Fuck you." Jax spits on the man's shoes, but this time he doesn't fight back.

A man is beside me. Pale blue eyes that seem somewhat concerned stare down at me. He's talking, but I can't register his words. All I can hear is the pounding of my own heart in my ears.

When he tries to pick me up, I fight him with what little energy I have left.

"Hey." The man grabs my shoulders and forces me to look at him. "We're here to help you."

I don't know what to believe, but I know I don't have the strength to keep fighting. My vision goes in and out of darkness, the sounds of angry voices the only anchor to consciousness.

"Get her out of here," someone orders.

Weightless, I know I'm being carried. I try to fight the darkness, but in the end, I let it consume me.

Chapter 15

Keeley

I wake up suddenly, my heart jackhammering in my chest.

A shadowed figure looms over me, and I immediately panic.

"You're safe." Henry's thick, rich voice croons, as his hand reaches out and brushes against my cheek.

"Henry?" His name comes out as a croak, and my hands immediately go to my throat, which feels raw and bruised.

"Here." He helps me sit, and passes me a glass of water.

I sip slowly, trying to put the pieces of what happened together. My entire body feels like I've been in a train wreck.

Jax – he did this to me. But the other men? Where had they come from? And how did I get back to Henry's apartment?

I feel like I've fallen down the rabbit hole, and ended up on the wrong side of the looking glass. Nothing makes sense.

"How…" I swallow painfully. "How did I get here?"

Henry stands over me, eyes narrowed and I can almost feel the tension radiating off him. He's angry. Really angry.

"My men brought you back." He shoves his hands in his pant pockets and stares down at me, like he's daring me to fight him.

It's then that I realize what he's saying.

"Your men?" The guys who stormed into Jax's place. That's who he's talking about. They belonged to him? But how did he know where I was? It hits me like a sledgehammer to the skull, and I shake my head, blinking up at him. I don't want to believe it. "You had me followed?"

"Yes." His answer is blunt, and holds no apology.

I let it sink in and fresh panic starts to creep its way up my throat as Jax's words come back to me – *You think that Henry Caldwell would be with someone like you if it wasn't for some gain?*

I bite my lip, and flinch when he reaches out to touch my face.

He drops his hand, and a pained expression crosses his face.

"Get some rest. We'll talk more later." He straightens and turns towards the door.

That's it? He's just going to drop the bomb that he had people following me, then leave?

"Wait."

He goes still, hand on the door handle, and turns slightly. I can see the muscle on his jaw bunch. His face is a mask, and I can tell he's trying to hold back his anger.

But who the hell is he to be upset with me?

I wince inwardly when I remember the note. But I don't owe him an explanation. This was never going to be more than a one-night-stand. No matter how much I wish otherwise. It just lasted a week longer than it should have.

"What, Keeley?" His dark eyes drill into me, and my entire body warms from the look he gives me.

I shake my head and look away.

"Nothing," I whisper.

A harsh, unsteady growl rolls across the room, and I startle, glancing up at the man who looks ready to devour me.

The sad thing is I know I'd be completely helpless if he chose to do so.

After a long, tense moment, his nostrils flare. When he speaks next, his voice is low and deep, and each word is edged with a possessiveness that sends a shiver down my spine.

"Don't run from me again."

His eyes are locked on mine, and he doesn't break his gaze until I give a small nod.

I can't even process the emotions that are spinning through me. Fear. Confusion. Anger. Hurt. And the most confusing, *need*.

Tears blur my vision as I watch him walk out of the room. Despite all my questions, I want to call him back, beg him to wrap his arms around me, to hold me. Only in his embrace do I feel safe, protected.

It's insane. Because for all I know, he's the one I need protection from.

Jax's words continue to haunt me. *The man fucked your sister. Got her pregnant. Killed herself because of him.*

Is that why Henry wants me? As some sick, twisted retribution for what he did in the past?

I lie back in bed and run my hands over my face. I don't how much of what Jax said I should believe.

One thing I've learned over the years is that there's *always* a touch of truth in every lie. And there's no denying that Henry knew Abby.

Don't believe me, ask him, Jax's words taunt.

I have every intention to.

Chapter 16

Henry

A cold, hard knot of rage forms in the pit of my stomach and my jaw aches with the force of my teeth grinding together as I listen to Michael's recap of what went down.

"The guy's name is Jax Williams." Michael sighs and places a thick folder on the island counter in front of me. "Low level drug dealer. Couple arrests on his record. Spent time in foster care and juvie."

I open the folder and let out a low breath, frustration brewing inside me when I recognize the bastard from the club.

The fact that Keeley went running to him isn't lost on me. I saw the texts, I know why she went, but she also had to trust the man enough to believe he was telling the truth. She hasn't said much about their relationship, but she also hasn't denied that they had one.

Jealousy all but consumes me.

"Did he talk?"

"Yeah. We got what we needed before the cops took him away." Michael's green eyes flash with something I haven't seen in years – concern.

"What?"

"He isn't the only one after the girl. Whatever her brother is into, it goes deeper than just drugs."

"Fuck." I toss the file on the counter, then rub my hand over the back of my neck. "Any idea where he's hiding?"

"Williams thinks he's skipped town."

"Fucking coward," I mumble under my breath. That Keeley risked herself for the bastard's life, when he clearly has no concern for hers, makes my blood boil. "I want you to find him."

"Working on it, boss." Michael's hawk-like gaze doesn't waver from me, and I know he's not telling me something. But how much worse can the situation get?

"Spit it out."

Michael sighs and leans against the wall, thick arms crossed over his chest. "You were right about Sullivan."

Shit.

I place my palms on the counter and brace for what I already know. "Tell me."

"He did a good job covering his tracks. But if I had to guess, John Sullivan is the girl's father."

Pinching the bridge of my nose, I start to pace. "And the mother?"

Michael pulls out a folded sheet of paper from his jacket pocket and places it in front of me. "It's bad."

My fingers shake when I read the headline printed on the newspaper clipping – *Mother kills infant, then herself. Two oldest children escape.*

I scan the article, then the date. Keeley would have been about six when it happened. "And Sullivan?"

"From what I can tell, after the incident he stopped all financial aid. The kids were placed in foster care. Bounced from home to home, before they aged-out."

I crush the paper in my fist, and fight the urge to go to Keeley. I can't even begin to imagine the nightmares she's lived through. Fury all but consumes me when I think of the fucker Sullivan leaving his own children in the hands of strangers.

The bastard won't get away with it. I'll make sure he pays for what he's done. After all the grief he gave me over Abby, and he practically did the very thing he accused me of.

Memories from the past start to make sense. I start to wonder if my father didn't know the truth the entire time. The beatings I got for insisting what I saw that day, they make sense, if he was trying to cover up for John.

"I want everything you've got on Sullivan and Keeley's mom. If I'm going to expose what he's done—"

"It's true." Keeley stands in the kitchen doorway, eyes wide in her pale face. "I didn't believe Jax when he told me."

She shakes her head and looks at me like I'm somehow responsible for all her suffering, and I have no idea why.

Even in the dim evening light, I can see the dark bruises around her neck, the paleness of her skin. I take three long strides towards her, but she draws back when I reach out to touch her. What the fuck?

"I don't know what Jax told you, but I'm trying to help. If my men hadn't found you, who knows what that bastard would have done."

She snorts, and her lips curl back in a sneer. "At least he didn't lie to me. Didn't pretend to be interested in me, and for what?" She jabs her finger at my chest. "Was it a revenge fuck? Or you screwed the one sister, so you had to have the other?"

"Careful," I warn, feeling my own temper flare. What the hell had the bastard told her?

"No, you be careful. Cause I'm not buying this whole white knight thing you're selling."

Michael coughs behind me, and we both turn and glare at him.

"I'm going to head out. I'll call you when I have more information."

I give a sharp nod. We both stare at each other in silence until Michael is gone.

Tears gather in Keeley's eyes, and her chin trembles slightly. I want to pull her into my arms, make everything better. But at the same time, I want to shake her until she realizes that I'm not the bad guy here.

She tilts her head and blinks up at me like she's come to some God-awful conclusion.

"Jax was right. You've been using me this entire time."

If I hear the asshole's name on her lips one more time, I may end up putting my fist through a wall.

111

"And *how* exactly am I using you?" My back teeth grind together, and I practically hiss the words. I see her flinch, but I don't fucking care. I'm pissed. I lean into her and demand, "I want to know exactly what I'm being accused of."

She pushes past me and opens a drawer, pulling out a manila envelope, then dumps the pictures on the counter in front of me. "You're not the only one who knows things."

I glance down at the pile of scattered photos. It's been years since I've looked at them. I'm not even sure why I've kept them all this time, other than to torment myself with guilt.

Kneeling, I pick up the single photo that fell on the floor. I stare down at it, then brush my fingers across the matte outline of Abby's face. The photo was taken the summer before our senior year, around the same time she started hooking up with the bastard that ultimately destroyed her.

I still don't know the asshole's name, or even what he looked like. Abby never told me. She was smart not to, because I probably would have killed the bastard if I'd found out.

"Whatever you think you know, you're wrong." I place the picture beside the others.

"Then tell me. Give me some good explanation for all this." She gestures to the photos. "Tell me the truth."

Tell her the truth. I could. Maybe I even should. But I made a promise on Abby's grave that I wouldn't mar her memory.

"It's complicated."

"Right." She rolls her eyes and crosses her arms over her chest defensively. "But you knew who I was all this time. That she was my sister."

"No." I swallow hard, realizing it's a lie. "Shit. Maybe. I don't know."

"You don't know?"

"I had my suspicions when I was in your apartment that first night."

"But you didn't say anything?"

"Like I said, it was only a feeling. I wanted to make sure before I said anything. I didn't even know if you knew about her–"

"I didn't. Not until today when Jax showed me her obituary." A tear slides down her cheek and she brushes it away angrily.

"God, Keeley. I'm so sorry."

She puts her hand up to stop me from reaching out and touching her.

"Just tell me the truth. This thing between us, it's all been about her?"

"No." It comes out sounding more like a growl than a word, and I see her blink in surprise.

"But you were in a relationship?"

"It's complicated. And it was a long time ago. It doesn't change anything that's between us."

"It changes everything."

I grind my teeth knowing I need to tell her the truth, or I'm going to lose her.

"Were you in love with her?"

"No." It's the truth. There had never been anything romantic between Abby and I. Not that she wasn't gorgeous, but she was like a sister to me. "I loved her. But I wasn't in love with her. We were just friends."

"Friends?" She looks at me like she doesn't believe me.

"Our families were close. We vacationed together, so Abby and I were pretty much glued at the hip, until–" I clench my jaw and look away from Keeley's accusing gaze.

"Until what?"

"Until I fucked up."

Keeley's eyes widen, and I know she's thinking the worst. God only knows what conclusions she's come to, or what lies that bastard told her. I'm still trying to figure out how he even knows about Abby, and what his motivation was to tell Keeley about her.

"What did you do?" The question seems forced from her lips, like she doesn't really want to know the answer.

"I didn't protect her the way I should have." I place my palms on the counter and close my eyes. As soon as I do, an image of Abby lying in my arms, lips blue, eyes vacant, blasts into my head like a horror movie replaying itself over and over again. "She needed my help, and I wasn't there for her."

Silence hangs between us, and I can feel Keeley's gaze on me, but with the guilt heavy on my shoulders, I can't look up. Seeing the blame in her eyes will all but gut me now.

"So you're trying to make up for it? Is that what this has all been about?"

"No."

"I'm trying to figure out what you want from me?"

"Nothing more than you're willing to give. I've waited twenty years to find you, I can't lose you now."

"Twenty years?" Her brows furrow, and I can almost see her mind racing.

So she doesn't remember. Not that I'm surprised. She was young and it was ages ago. But the fact that she kept the sword all these years. It has to mean something.

I move around the counter and open the drawer, pulling out the child's toy.

"I thought when you left it with the note that maybe you remembered."

"Remember what?"

I run my fingers over the carving on the handle. "H.W.C."

She frowns, but takes the sword when I hand it to her.

"They're my initials. Henry William Caldwell. This was mine."

"Yours?" Something flashes beneath the brilliant blue gaze as it holds mine.

"You were sitting under a tree, crying when I found you. You were dirty, and there were bruises covering your arms and legs. I don't remember much about the day, but I always remembered your eyes. The clearest blue." This time when I reach out to stroke her cheek, she doesn't finch away.

She shakes her head, but I know it's more from shock than denial.

"The woman you were with, she was arguing with John Sullivan. I didn't understand what it was about then. I just knew I wanted to keep you safe."

115

"From dragons," she whispers. Her eyes are closed and there's a slight tremble to her bottom lip. "I remember."

"I wanted to find you after you left, but when I told my father what happened–" I wince, remembering the beating I'd received when I'd told him what I'd seen. I hadn't been able to sit down for nearly a week afterwards. "I wasn't allowed to talk about what I saw. I'm sorry."

"You're the knight?" She blinks up at me, tears welling in her eyes. "I dreamed of you. For years, I believed you'd find me."

"I did find you." I cup my hand around the back of her neck and gently pull her towards me. For a moment, I feel her melt against me. "And this time I'm not going to let you go."

"No." She shakes her head and takes a step back, dropping the sword into my hands. "It doesn't change anything."

I move in front of her when she starts towards the door.

"I'm not the bad guy here."

"Maybe not. But I'm not going to be a pawn in whatever game you're playing."

I narrow my gaze. "I'm not playing games, Keeley."

"Then why did you have me followed?" Her voice cracks and I can tell it hurts for her to speak. "Why all the secrets?"

"Because you won't tell me a damn thing. If you trusted me, I wouldn't have to go digging."

"Bullshit. You probably had your men looking into my past the moment we met. You think that's normal? It's insane. This whole situation is crazy. So unless I'm your prisoner now, I'm asking you to leave me alone, let me go."

"No fucking chance in hell." All the anger I've been holding in for the past hour boils to the surface. "You need my help, and I'm not letting you walk away when there are people out there who want to hurt you. You might not like it, but we're bound together. And I'm going to make bloody well sure that *no one* ever hurts you again."

Her nostrils flare and I can almost see the walls she's building around herself – a steel cage. Her breathing has slowed, and the look she gives me is deadpan.

"Just because I decided to sleep with you doesn't give you any power over me." Her voice is low, steady, but I can tell every word she utters takes every ounce of strength she has left. "And don't pretend like there's anything more than sex between us."

Her words are like a smack to the face. I know she's hurting, that she's confused, but for a moment I actually think she believes it.

"Fine." I shove my hands in my pockets and narrow my gaze. "You want to walk out that door." I tilt my head towards the exit. "Go ahead."

"I will," she says coldly, but there's a hesitation in her voice and she doesn't move.

"Then go."

I can see the uncertainty in her eyes, the vulnerability and despair. It's all I need. Because even if she tried I know there's no way in hell I'm letting her walk away.

With three long strides, I bridge the gap between us and wrap one arm around her waist, the other hand behind her neck, forcing her to look at me.

"Let me go," she whispers halfheartedly. Her gaze rests on my mouth and her tongue pokes out, running across her bottom lip.

A low rumble catches in my throat, and I'm unable to stop myself from what I do next. I drop my mouth to hers, crushing her lips against mine, knowing that with the kiss I'm taking the last remaining fight from her. It's dirty using her attraction for me as gain. But right now, I don't fucking care. She's mine, and she needs to remember it.

"You don't want to leave," I growl against her lips.

"No," she whimpers, hands resting on my chest. "But I know I should."

I can tell the admission takes everything from her.

"Stay." It's not a request. I'm not giving her that option.

When she nods, I know I've won. She may not fully trust me, and that damn steel cage is back up around her heart, but at least she's still here, in my arms, and as long as she is with me, I know there's still hope for us.

Chapter 17

Keeley

"Keeley, look at me." His fingers graze my cheek, soft, yet so full of power and possession that it's impossible to turn away.

My entire body melts into his, seeking the warmth and protection he's offering. I hate how defenseless I am around him.

I try to resist the heat that pours through my veins, the desire that pools between my thighs, but it's no use.

"This is insane. Everything that's happened…" I shake my head, feeling like my entire world has been flipped upside down. "I don't know what to do."

"You're going to let me take care of things. Take care of you." Despite the gentleness of his tone, there's a certainty in his voice that doesn't leave room for argument.

I've never been one to let other people take control, and no matter how easy it would be to let him, I just can't.

"I don't need anyone–"

He stops my words with a single look, brows raised, gaze steady.

"Everyone needs someone, Keeley. Even you. It's not weakness to let people help you." He places his palm on my cheek and I can't help but rest against it.

Maybe he's right. Or maybe I just want to believe him because I'm so freaking tired, physical and mentally.

A small yawn escapes my lips.

"Come on. Let's get you back to bed."

His hand rests on the small of my back, and when he starts to lead me back to his bedroom, I don't resist.

So many questions flood my head. There's still so much that we have to talk about, but I don't know where to start. And right now, I'm too tired to even form a cohesive thought.

"Get undressed," he orders, pulling one of his large t-shirts from his dresser. "You're not sleeping in your clothes."

I pull my shirt over my head and take the t-shirt he offers. Henry helps me with my jeans, then pulls the comforter down.

Tears prick the back of my eyes and I don't know why.

"Hey," he says, reaching out, wiping away the tear that falls over my cheek. I try to turn my head away, but he doesn't let me. "Everything's going to be all right, sweetheart."

"You don't know that."

"This is where you belong. With me. I swear to God I'm going to keep you safe." He cups my chin and forces me to look at him. "Just promise you won't run again."

It's a big promise. One I'm not sure I can make. "Henry…"

He smiles sadly, then kisses my forehead.

I lean into his chest, resting my head just below his chin, and his arms wrap solidly around me. *Warmth and strength.*

"I won't run from you," I whisper, looking up at him. "Just don't keep things from me."

He presses a kiss to my hair and I can feel him nod. "Okay."

"Okay," I repeat, knowing it goes both ways. If he's really going to help me, I need to be honest as well. Tell him everything I know. I take a deep breath, then say wearily, "Drew owes money. A lot of it."

"I know."

I shake my head. "No, it's worse than I thought. I don't know how he did it, or why, but it isn't just the money he stole from Jax."

"I said I know. And I'll take care of it."

I pull back, frowning. "Take care of it how?"

"I have money, Keeley. *A lot of it.*" His lips twist up, but there's no humor in his eyes, only resolve. "We'll pay off his debt, and once he's safe, we'll get your brother into a good rehab center. Make sure this shit never happens again."

It's more than I expected. More than Drew deserves. And even though my initial urge is to fight him on it, I know this is my only hope.

"Thank you," I whisper.

He kisses my forehead, then ushers me into bed, pulling the covers over me once I lay down.

"You need to sleep, and I need to make a few phone calls."

I grab his hand. "Wait."

"Do you need me to get you something?"

"Just you," I croak, the words coming out more desperate than I intended. But God it's the truth. I need him more than my next breath, more than the very air I breathe.

His eyes go dark, and he gives a small knowing nod. "Okay."

Relief floods through me. I don't want to be alone right now.

His deft fingers meticulously working their way down the buttons of his shirt. In the dim light, the shadows cut deep, defined edges in each of his muscles. He's so damn gorgeous, I can't help but stare.

"You can always have me, Keeley." His gaze is locked on mine, as he unbuckles his belt. "I'm yours."

Mine. The thought makes my insides turn to liquid heat. *My knight.* A small chill races up my spine remembering the promises he made me twenty years ago.

He crawls into bed beside me, gloriously naked, and lays on his back, pulling me against his chest. I expect him to take me, but instead he just holds me, like the first night we met. Patient and gentle. Thinking more about my own needs than his own.

I rest my head in the nook of his shoulder and listen to the steady sound of his breathing.

"I'm lost in you," I admit. *So completely lost that I don't know if I'll ever find my way out.*

He shifts slightly, so that he can see my face. "Is that a bad thing?"

"I'm not sure." If he ever decided to walk away, it would break me. I trail my fingers over each one of his defined abs. "The past week has been a whirlwind. I don't know what's real and what's not."

He tilts my chin with his thumb and presses a soft kiss on my forehead.

"This–" He kisses my nose. "Is–" Then his lips are on mine, and he all but growls the last word against my mouth, "Real."

"Yes," I moan, needing the confirmation of his words, the confirmation of his body. My hands run over the tense muscles of his back, fingers clawing at him, wanting him closer.

"You need sleep," he says huskily, his teeth raking against the curve of my jaw, down my neck.

"I need *you.*"

He tenses for a brief moment, then lets out a low guttural growl. "Good."

A second later, my t-shirt is off, his hands are buried in my hair, and his lips are possessing mine with a hunger so fierce I feel consumed by it.

The kiss burns through my senses, and I'm desperate to hold onto the bond between us.

This is real. His words undo me, and make me want to surrender completely. He said he's mine, but I know the truth, *I'm his.*

Each kiss, each touch, only confirms what I already know. He's marked me. Mind, body and soul. With or without him, I'll never be the same again.

Henry nips at my lips, a harsh groan rumbling in his throat. Then his mouth slides from mine, rasping down my neck, to my breasts, focusing on the tight, sensitive peak of my nipples. His hands stroke up my thighs, my hips, my ass, each caress pulling me deeper into a vortex of pleasure.

He's between my legs, his hard cock wedged between my thighs, and I'm almost dripping with need to have him inside of me. I lift my hips, trying to get closer.

"Not yet." He pushes my thighs further apart, but instead of sinking deep inside me, he lowers himself. Pure, wicked lust gleaming in his eyes as he descends between my legs.

"Henry," I say his name as a desperate plea.

A moan of tortured pleasure rushes from my lips when his tongue lashes out across my clit. I swear I'm so close to coming that the room seems almost alive with the energy pulsing between us.

"What do you need, Keeley?" His fingers move up my thigh, stroking the sensitive flesh. "Tell me what you need and I'll give it to you."

"You," I cry out. Knowing I've lost myself in the confession. That part of me that I've always kept aloof, caged, and protected is open and vulnerable – *and his*. "I need all of you."

He moves quickly, and with a single hard thrust, buries himself inside me.

"You have me." His hands grip my wrists, pulling them above my head, as he pulls out, then sinks in slowly, filling me completely, so that our bodies are molded together.

We stay like that for a few moments, gaze locked together, nothing separating us. My heart beats faster as I stare into his eyes, overwhelmed by the dark, shadowed emotions I see there.

"I love you, Keeley," he says, resting his forehead against mine and closing his eyes. "You've been mine since the moment we first met."

I suck in a breath. I've never believed in the illusion of love. Lust, yes, but not love. My mouth opens, then shuts on the words I know he wants me to return. It's too soon. There are still so many things I don't know about him. Things that could change everything between us.

"Henry–"

"I don't need you to say it back." He nips at my bottom lip, and gives a small thrust, making me moan. "This is enough – *for now.*"

His lips are on mine, tongue slipping past, and he lunges deeper inside of me. Each hard thrust reinforcing his words. *I love you.*

I've never been loved before. Not really. Not by my parents, not by Jax, not even by Drew. I can't even remember a time when someone said the words to me. Maybe when I was little, but whatever my mom felt for me, it was anything but love.

I cling to Henry, wanting to believe in his promises, wanting to believe in *us.*

His hips slam into mine, flesh pounding against flesh, and I can feel the rise of my orgasm building within me. Tremors race through my body, and a strangled cry erupts from my throat.

A shattering explosion rips through my body, sending me blindly over the edge, and I clench around him until I feel him coming hard inside of me.

It isn't until I feel hot semen between my thighs that I realize we forgot to use a condom.

Chapter 18

Henry

I rise quietly from the bed, careful not to wake Keeley. She fell asleep in my arms moments after we finished making love, and hasn't stirred for the past few hours. I hate leaving the warmth of her body, but I still need to talk to Michael to see what else he's learned.

Running my fingers through my hair, I glance down at her, hoping to hell she's not going to be pissed that we didn't use protection. I'm never that fucking irresponsible, but if I'm honest with myself I didn't want anything between us. I never want anything between us again.

She's on the pill, I've seen the little package in her make-up bag, and we're both clean. But I know we still have to talk about it when she wakes up.

I pull on a pair of cotton pajama bottoms and a t-shirt, then move into the kitchen, flicking on the lights. The sky is still dark, but I reach for my phone and dial Michael's number.

"It's late," Michael's grizzly voice says on the other end.

I glance at the clock and wince. "Or early, depending on how you look at it."

He huffs. "I sent you an email with the files and reports."

"And?"

"That bastard, Jax Williams, was right. The kid racked up over a hundred grand in debt. Most of it under the table."

"I want it paid off."

"You sure you want to do that, boss? The minute these guys know the kid has a benefactor, there's no saying what–"

"This isn't just about the kid. I don't want anything that could threaten Keeley."

"We can keep her safe."

I blow out a breath, knowing he's right, but also knowing that Keeley would never forgive me, or herself, if anything happened to her brother.

"Just pay it off."

"All right." I hear the creak of the bed in the background, then a few seconds later the tapping of a keyboard. "It'll be done today."

"Good."

"There's something else I found that I didn't add to the report, but I thought you should know. I checked into the medical reports."

"And?" I grit my teeth, hearing the concern in his voice.

"And there's multiple references to personality disorder, bipolar, possible schizophrenia."

"She killed her own kid, that's not really surprising."

"I wasn't talking about the mother. It seems that Drew was flagged early on, which is one of the reasons he was shipped between so many homes. Behavioral issues, social anxiety, aggression, mental instability…it goes on. I know you probably don't want to hear this, but the file on the kid, it's pretty similar to the one on Abby."

"Don't."

"You need to hear this," Michael says tersely. "Personality disorders are often genetic. If he is John Sullivans kid, then–"

"I said don't," I growl into the phone, fingers tightening painfully around the receiver.

"You read Abby's report." His voice is low, calm, as if to placate me, but all I can hear is a roaring in my ears as tension builds inside my head. "You know what her therapists said. She was suffering from delusions for months, maybe years before she took her own life."

"If there was something wrong with her, I would have known." It was just another way for her parents to shift the blame onto someone or something else. Sure, she was a bit quirky, and she had some anxiety, but nothing like her parents tried to make it out to be.

Michael sighs heavily on the other end. "I'll send you the report. Take a look at it."

"I will," I say, praying to God that he's wrong. "Just find the kid, so we can get him whatever help he needs."

"And Sullivan? What do you want me to do about him?"

"Nothing for now." I rub my temples and close my eyes. As much as I want to expose the bastard,

doing so will only bring unwanted attention to
Keeley.

"Becca's wedding is next weekend," Michael says
evenly. "You saw the guest list?"

"Shit." I'd forgotten the Sullivans were invited.
"I'll deal with it."

I hang up and immediately send a text to Becca,
demanding that she remove them from the list.
Because there's no way I'm going to let Keeley spend
even a second in that man's presence.

Chapter 19

Keeley

Rolling over in bed, I frown at the empty spot beside me. Golden light streaks through the blinds and the smell of coffee, the soft hum of the television drift through the small crack in the door.

A small smile tugs at my lips, as I remember his words. *I love you.*

Three words that could change everything if I let them.

But there's so much I still don't know, so much that needs to be resolved.

There's no question I'm falling for him – hard. That's not the issue. The real question is whether I can trust him.

Like love, trust isn't something I give away easily. I've endured loss and survived. But surviving comes at a cost, and although my scars are hidden inside me, they're still there.

Every person I've ever loved, I've lost. Even Drew, if I'm honest with myself.

Sadness swells inside me.

You don't have to be alone. The devastatingly gorgeous man in the next room, he can be mine. *Mine.*

Warmth floods through me – until I try to stand. Every muscle in my body protests, and images of Jax's hands around my throat assault me. His powerful presence crushing me against his weight. The look of pure hatred in his eyes. The beautiful, broken boy turned into a monster of a man.

There was a time when I wanted to save him. But I finally realized that some wreckage isn't salvageable. Sometimes you only have enough strength to save yourself.

Jax never forgave me for leaving. Neither did Drew. Even after I'd distanced myself, Drew could never see Jax for what he is – a criminal.

I blame myself for staying as long as I did. Maybe if I'd made a clean break sooner, Drew wouldn't have gotten caught up in the drug scene. Maybe he wouldn't be in hiding now. Maybe Jax wouldn't be after us both.

Fear closes in like a dark shroud, the warmth I felt earlier, gone.

I dress in an old gray hoodie and black stretch pants, and wince when I catch my reflection in the mirror. Dark circles under my eyes match the angry bruises around my neck. I swallow hard, and force a smile on my face.

The minute I open the bedroom door, I hear a woman's raised voice, and Henry's frustrated, muffled response.

I make my way down the long hall towards the living room where the shouting is coming from.

"You're trying to ruin my wedding," Becca says, arms crossed her chest, large tears streaming down her cheeks, somehow not smudging her perfectly applied makeup.

"You don't even care if they're there." Dressed in a white t-shirt that stretches over his muscular chest, and a pair of ripped jeans that hang low on his waist, Henry runs his fingers through his dark hair and lets out a frustrated sigh. "All you want is to make that bastard happy."

"That bastard is going to be my husband." Becca hiccups on a small sob, and covers her mouth with the back of her hand in an overdramatic gesture. "You're being unreasonable. You won't even tell me why you've changed your mind. If you really want me to take the Sullivans off the guest list, then give me one valid reason."

A small tremble of dread races down my spine.

The Sullivans are going to be at Becca's wedding?

I swallow hard, feeling moisture well in my eyes, the sudden sense that I'm being set in another trap.

"You invited me to the wedding, knowing my father was going to be there?" My voice is small, but they both turn, and I see Henry's face go pale.

"It's not what you think, Keeley." He moves quickly to my side, placing his hands on my shoulders.

"Your father?" Becca blinks, eyes wide, mouth open. She shakes her head. "I don't understand."

The unbearable weight of the last few days comes crashing down on me, and when I open my mouth to speak, no words come out.

"Shit, Keeley, look at me." His palms rest on the sides of my face. Dark eyes capture mine and pull me in. "I'm trying to make things right. Trust me."

Trust him. It's a choice I need to make. Either that or walk away. Because there's nothing in between.

"Would someone please tell me what's going on," Becca demands, twisting her hands, clearly agitated.

"Tell her," I whisper.

Henry places a chaste kiss on my forehead, then releases me and starts to pace.

Aware of Becca's wide-eyed gaze on me, I sit down on the sofa and curl into myself.

After a few tension-filled minutes, Henry says with disdain tainting his voice, "Keeley and her brother Drew are both John Sullivans kids."

"Holy shit." Becca continues to blink at me, shaking her head. "That's why you look so much like her, like Abby."

"Becca," Henry says sternly.

"It's okay." It makes sense now, the way she stared at me the first time we met. "You knew Abby?"

"Yes. She was like a sister to–" Becca's brows pinch. "I'm sorry. I didn't mean…"

"It's okay. I didn't even know about her until yesterday. I mean not really. I remember my mom talking about John's other child. But I never…" I swallow hard. "I never wanted anything to do with him or his other family."

"You don't talk to him?"

I shake my head, emotions stirring in my chest. Tension heavy, thick and suffocating like it always is whenever I think about the man who stole my childhood, who drove my mom to the brink of desperation.

Henry places a hand on my shoulder, and I immediately take it. *Strength and warmth.*

"My mom died when I was young. We didn't see him after that. He made sure no one knew about us." It's only half the story, but it's all she needs to know.

"Holy shit," she says again, eyes still wide, and I can tell she's still trying to process it. "I'm so sorry."

"Now you know why they can't be at the wedding," Henry says harshly.

"Of course. I'll tell Asher to take them off the list." Becca is still shaking her head, and I can see she wants to ask more questions.

"Thank you," Henry says. He pulls his phone from his pocket and curses. "I have to go in to the office. Will you be all right?"

I don't want him to leave. There's still so much we need to talk about, but I nod, and plaster a smile on my face. "Yes, of course."

He leans over and kisses my forehead, concern clear in his eyes.

"I'll stay with her," Becca blurts out. "I mean, as long as you don't mind."

"Sure." It's odd, but I actually prefer the company. I could use Becca's incessant chattering to keep my mind off Drew and everything else going on.

A muscle twitches in Henry's jaw. "There's a security team watching the place, and Michael–"

"I'll be fine."

He frowns, gaze boring into mine as if he can read all my fears like an open book. His fingers brush against my cheek with a tenderness that makes me want to weep.

"I'll be back in a few hours." When he drops his hand, I feel the loss of his touch through my whole body.

I watch him walk down the hall towards the elevator, hating being away from him for even that long.

"Security team?" Becca says with raised brows when Henry is gone.

"It's a long story." Subconsciously, my fingers move to my bruised neck. I drop them quickly when I see Becca's gaze drop.

"Good God, Keeley. What happened?"

"It's fine." I pull on my sweatshirt, trying to hide the marks.

"It doesn't look fine. It looks like someone tried to strangle you."

I shrug like it doesn't matter. I can't even imagine what she'll think of me if she knew everything. But in all honesty, I'm sick of hiding the truth. She's going to find out eventually, and there's a part of me that's desperate to talk to someone about it. Someone who isn't directly involved.

"Keeley?" She sits down beside me and places her hand on my arm.

"My brother's in trouble." I take a deep breath and rush through a quick snapshot of everything that's happened over the past couple of weeks.

When I'm done, Becca lets out a low whistle, her expression unreadable.

"I know how selfish I've been bringing Henry into all this." I start fidgeting with the strings on my hoodie, unable to meet Becca's blinking gaze. Guilt and panic threaten to rise like a storm inside me, and I do my best to push it down. "I understand if you don't want me near him. I know he deserves better. I tried to leave. So many times...but I can't."

"Because you're in love with him." Her eyes hold the hint of tears, despite the broad grin that stretches her face. "The way the two of you look at each other. It's obvious. I always wanted..." She shakes away whatever she was going to say, then places her hand on mine. "I'm glad you're here. And I'm glad Henry's making sure you're safe."

"Thank you."

In a heartbeat, I'm swept up into one of Becca's hugs.

"I should thank *you*. After what happened with Abby, I didn't think he'd ever be able to move on, but I see the change in him already, and–" Her fingers go to her lips and her eyes widen. "Shit, Keeley. I'm sorry. I shouldn't have mentioned her. Sometimes I just open my mouth and things come out."

"It's okay. It wasn't her fault what our father did." My mouth is dry, my palms sweaty, but I ask the question anyways. "Will you tell me about her?"

Her eyes pinch close. "She was Henry's age, so they spent more time together."

"They were close?" Tightness grips my chest, and I immediately regret asking the question.

"Yes." The word comes out as a rough murmur, almost pained. "Everyone always thought the two of them would get married."

137

My heart races and a knot of jealousy forms in the pit of my stomach. "They loved each other?"

"Very much, but not the way you're thinking." As if sensing my jealousy, she says, "I've never seen my brother look at a woman like he does you. It was just friendship between him and Abby."

"But…" Chewing on my nails, I debate whether or not to ask the next question. It's something I should talk to Henry about, but I don't know if I can handle hearing the truth from him. "She was pregnant?"

"Yes."

My chest squeezes painfully. So much for the *"just friends, theory."*

"What do you know?" Becca asks, pain stretched across her pretty face.

"Not much." I chew on my bottom lip. "Mostly just what her obituary said. That she took her own life."

Guarded, Becca searches my face, and I can tell there's things she doesn't know if she should tell me.

"People have been hiding things from me my entire life. I just want to know the truth."

On a heavy sigh, she gives a reluctant nod.

"Henry was obsessively protective of her, she was…" Emotions race across her features and sorrow creased the corners of her eyes. "Abby was always a little odd. Don't get me wrong. She was wonderful. Always the first to help. Always there if you needed her. But as she got older, things started to change. There were times when she'd say or do something that was completely out of character. Like she was becoming two different people. Henry never wanted to believe it. But we all saw what was happening."

I can't help but think about Drew. How similar Becca's description of Abby is. But Abby lived a perfect life. She had everything that Drew and I could only dream about. A family. A stable home.

"Is that why Henry left her?"

Becca's head snaps up. "Who told you that?"

"I-I just thought–" I stumble on my words, taken back by the horror in Becca's eyes.

"You thought wrong. Henry would never have left her. Ever."

"Then what happened?"

"You should talk to Henry." Her lips quiver at the corners, and I can hear the bitterness in her voice.

"Becca, please. I need to know." A spiral of doubt winds through me, but I push anyways.

"There were a lot of rumors." Sucking in a shaky breath, she continues, "Henry didn't care. His only thoughts were on helping Abby. But everyone believed the awful things they said about him. He's carried the guilt of her death around his neck like a noose for the past ten years. But it wasn't his fault." Her gaze narrows on me, and moisture pools there, her expression raw. "*Any of it.*"

I feel like there's so much more that she's not saying. I open my mouth to ask her, but she holds up her hand to stop me.

"You need to talk to Henry. It's his story. Not mine."

I don't push her further, and we sit in silence, both caught up in our own thoughts.

Do I really need to know everything? Becca's right, it's Henry's story to tell. It was a long time ago, and no matter what he did or didn't do, doesn't change who he is now.

Mine.

Chapter 20

Keeley

Alone in Henry's apartment, my cell phone feels like a fifty-pound weight in my hands. I re-read the text message for the tenth time and continue to pace.

I've found a way to make everything right.
Meet me at the coffee shop at the corner of Laurel St.
-D

A cold, sharp shiver races down my spine. *Drew.*

Relief mixes with apprehension. He's alive. That small fear that's been plaguing me eases.

I try to call the number back, but there's no answer, no machine, it just keeps ringing.

It's the first contact I've had from Drew since he went AWOL, and I can't ignore it. Henry will be pissed if I leave on my own, but I have to go.

Grabbing my purse, I race through the apartment and jam my thumb at the elevator button. On the way down, I try Henry's cell, then blow out a frustrated breath when he doesn't pick up.

I type a short text.

Drew contacted me.
Going to meet him.
Not running.

I type the last line, knowing it's what he'll think the moment his security team lets him know I've left the apartment.

As soon as the elevator doors open and I enter the atrium, I see two shadowy figures start towards me. The same two men that found me at Jax's apartment. One is on his phone, the other wears a scowl that would be intimidating if I didn't know they were hired for my protection.

I acknowledge them with a small nod, which is returned with deep frowns, then looks of startled surprise when I walk up to them.

"I assume you have orders to follow me?"

The larger of the two gives a sharp nod.

"Good." I don't know what to expect with Drew, and I may need them if he refuses to come back with me.

Without another word, I turn quickly and walk briskly out of the building, keeping a steady pace for the seven blocks it takes me to get to Laurel Street.

From the sidewalk outside the coffee shop, I see Drew. He sits at the back booth, dark hoodie pulled over his light brown hair.

He glances up when I walk towards him, his expression hard, desperate.

"You came," he says, blue eyes slightly glazed. But I don't know if it's from drugs, or lack of food and sleep, because he doesn't look like he's had much of either in the past two weeks.

His fingers tremble as he rips open a sweetener pack and pours it in his coffee.

Tension is thick, filling up the space between us.

My heart aches. Because the man in front of me is no longer the little boy that I used to know. Anger, drugs, life have beaten him down, and I wonder how much I really know him.

It doesn't matter though. He's still my baby brother. And I'll do anything to protect him.

I sit and accept the coffee the waitress brings me, waiting until she's gone to speak. "I've been worried sick about you."

Drew gives a small shrug, as if his disappearing act was nothing out of the ordinary.

"Jax said he told you everything." He takes a sip of his coffee, eyes darting around the coffee shop.

"You spoke with Jax?" My insides quake, heart sinking into my stomach. I place my palms on the table beside my mug and lean in, forcing Drew to look at me. "When?"

Drew all but shrinks into himself, like he's a child being reprimanded.

"When?" I say again, this time louder, making heads turn in our direction.

"He's going to help me."

"Help you?" I fist my fingers, and it's suddenly difficult to breathe.

143

"He figured out a way we can make everything better. You. Me. Him. We can leave. Get out of the city like you always wanted to do. We'll have enough money so you won't have to work anymore. And Jax can–"

"Drew, listen to me." It's difficult to speak with the panic clawing at my throat, but I'm able to force the words out. "Jax isn't trying to help you. Whatever he told you, it's a lie. He's using you to get to me."

"He was right," Drew snorts, blue eyes churning with anger, now directed at me. "You never believed in me. In him. All you care about is yourself."

"I care about you."

"Then help me."

"I'm trying to. Come with me. We can sort this out together. I promise."

"Come with *you*?" His once beautiful face twists in a sneer. "What, so that your boyfriend can call the cops on me, too? You want me locked up. Is that your plan?"

"No. Of course not." What had Jax told him?

Drew glances over my shoulder, eyes quickly filling with alarm, and one hand quickly snakes under his sweatshirt as if reaching for a weapon.

I look over my shoulder and see Henry's men saunter into the coffee shop, eyes trained on us.

"Those men are here to help us. To help *you*. Just come back with me. Everything will be all right. I promise."

He squeezes his eyes shut, and rubs the heel of his palm against his forehead, mumbling incoherently under his breath. When he looks at me again his expression is hard, tortured – *dangerous*. I've never been afraid of my brother before, but I am now.

"Jax was right, you've changed. You don't care about me. All you care about is that bastard you're shacking up with." His eyes are wild, darting around the room. His hand is still under his shirt, and I'm more certain than ever that he's carrying a weapon.

"You're wrong."

"I've got to get out of here."

"Drew, stop." I grab his free hand when he starts to shift on the bench, and he pulls it away like my touch burns him. My chest tightens and panic pulls at the edges of my mind, and my throat is so tight I can barely breathe. "Everything I've ever done has been to keep you safe. Look at me. Look in my eyes. I love you. Please don't run again. I can't help you if you do."

"I see you," he hisses, leaning towards me, lips pulled back exposing his teeth. His words are loud enough that people turn in their seats to watch us. "You're just like her. Like our mother. You're a selfish bitch who thinks about no one but herself."

"Drew." His name comes out on a breath.

"The man slept with our sister, fucked her and left. He'll do the same to you."

The entire coffee shop has gone eerily quiet and I can feel all eyes on me.

"You're wrong," I say softly, knowing I've already lost him.

"God, Keeley. You disgust me. I thought I knew you, but you'd rather be the man's whore than help your own brother. Like mother, like daughter, right?"

He spits on the ground beside the table, his eyes so black I can hardly see the rim of blue.

"Don't do this." A mass presses down on my chest, an excruciating weight almost too heavy to bear.

"You won't help me?" His own demons flicker across his face, hardening the edges so that I barely recognize him. "Then you're dead to me."

When he bolts from the table, I can't do anything but stare at the empty spot in front of me.

I sink into the depth of my misery, letting it consume me.

I'm not sure how long I sit there, minutes, hours. I sit there frozen. Unable or unwilling to move, I sink into myself, and choke down the sorrow that rises like a tidal wave, drowning all hope that everything would be okay.

I search inside myself, trying to steel my heart against the anguish that guts me, but I've let those walls down, and now I feel like I'm lying bleeding, exposed, with nothing to protect me.

Chapter 21

Henry

The second my driver comes to a stop in front of the small coffee shop, I open the door and jump out. Through the large glass windows, I can see Keeley sitting alone in a far booth. The shop is empty except for her and the two burly men that stand guard, watching her from a distance. It'll cost me to have the place shut down, but when Michael told me what happened, I wanted to give her privacy. I also didn't want to take the chance that Drew, or someone worse, might come back.

Michael meets me at the door and unlocks it.

"How is she?" I rake an agitated hand through my hair.

"Hasn't moved since the kid left," he says, looking worriedly over at Keeley. "Little shit did a number on her. And I'm pretty sure he was carrying." His lips curl in disgust. "I would have apprehended the motherfucker if I didn't have your orders not to hurt him. But the kid's a loose wire. Dangerous to himself and everyone around him."

"You did the right thing." The anger that I felt when I first got the call she'd left the apartment has sizzled, replaced by an aching need to get her home.

I make my way across the coffee shop and crouch beside her, taking her hand in mine, and bringing it to my lips. "Keeley?"

She blinks, and slowly turns her head towards me, her expression clouded.

"Let's go home."

"Drew...he..." Shivers roll through her and she closes her eyes.

"I know, sweetheart. I know."

A tear rolls down her cheek, and I capture it with my thumb.

"I-I can't help him."

"We'll still try. I promise." I thread her trembling fingers through mine.

She shakes her head, beautiful blue eyes brimming with despair, with a hopelessness I've never seen before.

My chest feels crushed by the pain I see there.

Haunted.

Broken.

So damned vulnerable.

Fuck, I wanted her walls to come down, but not like this.

I wrap my arms around her shoulders and help her from the booth. She doesn't resist. It's like all the fight has been ripped from her – and that scares me more than anything.

"Let's go home."

Chapter 22

Henry

Keeley shivers in my arms. She hasn't spoken since the coffee shop, just nods or shakes her head if I ask a question.

I lead her into the master bathroom and start the water in the large tub.

"Come here," I say, unbuttoning my shirt and letting it fall to the floor.

When she moves towards me, I help her out of her clothes. I expect her to protest, but she just follows my orders, expression distant, clouded.

I test the water, then help her in, slowly sinking in behind her, leaning back so that she's resting against my chest.

She relaxes against me, and I swear I can feel every ounce of pain she's feeling, like it's my own.

Fuck. What I wouldn't do to take it all away.

I rub the tight muscles of her shoulders and neck, and she lets out a deep breath, like she's been holding it in forever.

"I thought I could save him," she says quietly, lost in her grief.

I pull her hair behind her neck, wincing when I see the dark bruises, and press my lips against her temple. "You've done everything possible."

"Maybe," she says weakly. "Or maybe I didn't pay enough attention, didn't see the signs."

"This isn't your fault. None of it." I hold her a little tighter.

She shivers and I wonder what self-degrading thought passes through her mind. Because I know her, and I know that no matter what I say she's going to carrying Drew's burdens herself.

I know, because I've done the same thing with Abby. Carrying her sins around like they're my own. Never forgiving myself when it's her I'm really angry with. I see it now through Keeley's eyes, and the way she holds on to her brother like his choices are somehow in her hands.

A tightness that I've been carrying around for years suddenly releases and I let out a choppy breath. Maybe one day I'll gather the courage to tell Keeley everything. But now isn't the time. Not when she's still fighting her own guilt.

She curls into me, making the water slosh over the side of the tub. Her head rests on my chest, fingers trailing across my stomach.

Silence stretches between us, until she says, "Drew wanted me to go with him."

"Go where?"

"With Jax."

Every muscle in my body tenses, and I have to stop myself from snapping. What the fuck was the kid thinking?

"Does he know what that asshole did to you?"

"I don't know. I didn't have the chance to tell him. He just said he and Jax had a plan to pay back the money."

"Fucking hell." I can't hold back my anger. Sitting upright, I thread my fingers through my hair.

I see the silent tears rolling down her cheeks and regret my rough words.

"Shit. I'm sorry. Come here, sweetheart." She doesn't fight me when I pull her back against me, sliding back down into the warm water. I have my own views on what those two jackasses deserve, but I also made a promise that I would help her brother. "If we know that he's with Jax, then we know where he is, how to find him."

"He doesn't want to be found. That's the point. He said…" She gives a small sob that shakes her whole body, but she quickly reins back her emotions. "…that I'm dead to him."

Anger burns through my veins. After everything she's sacrificed for that little shit.

I take a deep breath.

"Desperation can make a person do and say horrible things." I run my hands down her arm, entwining my fingers with hers. "I know how important Drew is to you, will always be to you. But no matter what happens, you're not alone."

She gives a small shrug, like she doesn't believe me.

I turn her in my arms and capture her chin. "You've got me. I know you're not ready to accept everything that I want to give you. But I'm here for you. Whatever you need."

Her tongue darts out to wet her lips, then she whispers, "I want to trust you."

"Then trust me. Let me take care of you."

I gently draw my thumbs under her eyes, wiping away the mascara that smudged from her tears. Her eyes and lips are puffy and red from crying, but she's still the most beautiful thing I've ever seen.

"I won't let anyone hurt you. I'd die before I let that happen." I feel her shudder under my promise.

"My knight." She gives a smile that doesn't reach her eyes. Eyes so blue, they literally suck the breath from me every time she looks at me. But it's the pain I see there now that leaves me breathless. So much goddamn fear trembles through her.

"If you let me be."

God, I love her. More than I ever thought possible. So much that I would walk through the fires of Hades to put a smile on her face. To keep her safe, I would sacrifice so much more.

It's a ridiculous whirlwind of emotions, but they're as real as anything I've ever felt. But she's gripped a piece of my soul, made me long for things I hadn't known I wanted.

Silence swells around us, and I can practically feel all those vacant spaces inside her crying out to be filled. Even though she fights it, I know she needs me. Craves the protection I want to give her.

She's mine. I just need to find a way to make her trust me enough to allow herself to believe it.

When her gaze drops to my lips, I know what she wants – a distraction from the pain.

I pick her up and carry her to the bedroom, placing her in the middle of the bed.

So fucking gorgeous. Aphrodite would be jealous.

"Let go, sweetheart. Let me love you."

"You make me weak."

My heart breaks for the pain I hear in her voice.

"Only because you won't let go. Together we're stronger. I'll be your strength and you'll be mine."

"I can't."

"You will." I hold myself above her and slowly lower my lips to hers.

Her breath is warm against my mouth, like a whisper of heat.

"Touch me," she whispers, eyes bright with unspoken emotion. An array of emotions swirl behind her blue eyes. Sadness. Desire. Hope. Fear. "Please. Make the pain go away."

She's so close to giving me everything, and I can tell it scares her.

I fight the urge to push her, knowing it will be so much better when she gives it freely.

"Make love to me," she whispers, fingers tangling in my hair, pulling me towards her. But I can see the hesitation behind the blue-depth. A ridiculous belief that she's somehow tainted, unworthy.

My heart aches for the need to make her see herself the way I see her.

Beautiful.

Cherished.

Perfect.

"Everything feels better when you're touching me," she whimpers.

"I never want to stop touching you. I can barely breathe for the want of it. You make me so fucking hard I can barely think straight." I lower my head and nip at her lower lip, nudging her thighs apart with my knee.

She lifts her hips towards me and her thighs wrap around my hips, drawing me in. Her arms tighten around my neck, and her mouth is on mine, hungry and desperate.

"So fucking perfect," I groan, sipping at her lips, rather than devouring them.

"I want to taste you," she whispers breathlessly, hands running down my chest, abs. "I want you in my mouth." Her fingers surround my cock, stroking it. "Please."

I groan, rolling over on my back when she pushes against my chest.

She licks her lips, staring down at me as she kneels between my legs and wraps her fingers around the engorged shaft.

Lowering her head, her tongue licks over the tip. A rasp of breath leaves my chest, and my cock jerks against her sweet lips.

"Fuck, Keeley." My hands are in her hair, guiding her down as she takes every fucking inch of me. "Christ. Your mouth, sweetheart. So damn good."

"You like that?" Her eyes are all innocence, as if she doesn't know she's rocking my entire world.

"God, yes."

My muscles tighten and bunch each time she flicks her tongue over the crest, then sucks me deeper. Teasing. Stroking. Licking. Until I'm ready to explode in her mouth.

Fire races up my spine, each stroke of her tongue a lash of agonizing pleasure.

"Keeley, shit." I tug at her hair gently. "Stop, or I'm going to come too soon."

She blinks up at me and releases my cock, a small smile curving her lips.

"If that's what it takes to make you smile, you can do that all day long," I tease, flipping her on her back.

"I wouldn't mind." She grins, digging her hands in my hair and guiding my head between her legs. "But I like this too."

"I know you do." I lick at her inner thigh, trailing my tongue along the sensitive flesh. *Fucking heaven.* No other woman had ever tasted so sweet.

She's so wet, so hot, it would be so easy to slide between her thighs and fuck her hard and deep. First, I want her shuddering in ecstasy against my lips, my tongue, crying out my name with the pleasure of it.

I cup her ass, lifting her to me, parting her silken folds with my tongue. Licking. Nipping. Kissing. She trembles against me, my tongue working until she's on the brink of losing all control.

"Yes," she moans, her voice a tight rasp. Her head tilts back, eyes closed, a look of pure rapture crossing her features.

I grip her hips, thrusting my tongue deeper, savouring the sweet taste of her orgasm.

She tenses, shudders, then goes limp with a small whimper of pleasure still on her lips.

"Henry." Eyes closed, breath uneven, she murmurs my name in a post-orgasmic haze.

I kiss her stomach, fingers brushing across her nipples, moving between her thighs, I let out a harsh groan as her slick, sweet flesh encases the crest of my cock. She stretches around me, her thighs opening, hips arching.

I go still above her, muscles bunched and knotted. I can feel the inferno building, making my balls tighten.

"Look at me, sweetheart."

She blinks, giving me a half-lidded smile, a glazed look of hunger and need filling her eyes.

My chest squeezes at the emotions that stir there. *Damn.* I've never known this feeling for any other woman. Tenderness. Lust. A possessiveness that burns to the depth of my soul.

Beneath me, she moves her hips, her body begging for more.

I pull out slowly, so that only the engorged crest of my cock fills her. She moans as if in pain, and I thrust back deeper than I'd been before. She cries out and clenches tight around me, pleas for relief tumbling from her sweet mouth.

Buried deep inside her, I lose my last ounce of control.

My heart thunders.

My breathing speeds.

My cock is harder than it's ever been.

Her mouth parts on a moan, and I press my lips against hers, catching the cry of pleasure that tears from her throat. I feel the first waves of her orgasm wrapping around my cock, tearing through my senses.

An eruption of white-hot heat pierces through me, and I moan low and ragged, the pleasure too much. I explode within her, each pulse of my release matched by her own small spasms.

It isn't just lust. It's so much more. Beyond pleasure. Beyond ecstasy. This woman is my heart. My fucking soul.

Shattered and damaged, but still *mine*.

Now I just have to find a way to heal her.

Chapter 23

Keeley

I toss and turn, kicking at the covers that are wrapped too tight around my body. A cold sweat breaks out across my skin, and pure terror sweeps through me like a dark entity sent to consume and destroy my soul. A prisoner to the dreams that would forever keep their hold. Always there, always threatening. Drew. Lily. Jax. My mom – But it's Henry's face I see this time. Laughing and mocking as I fall through the black void that devours me.

"Keeley. Wake up." Henry's voice pulls me from the nightmare, but the minute I wake up, nausea rolls over me. He wipes the damp hair off my forehead while I count to ten in my head, praying that my stomach will settle.

"I'm okay," I say, placing my palm on his face, and wishing I wasn't the cause of the concern I see on it.

"The nightmares are getting worse."

He's right. They are. But they aren't just nightmares. They're memories. So vivid they tear open the wound on my soul, making me sink deeper into the fortress I've built around myself.

"It's fine. I'm fine," I lie, wiggling out of his embrace and sitting up. Immediately I regret the action. My head spins, my stomach revolts and sweat slickens my skin. I place my hands on the edge of the bed, feet on the floor, ready to bolt to the bathroom if I need to.

I can't be sick. Not for Becca's wedding.

"Shit, Keeley, you're white as a ghost." Henry practically jumps across the bed to crouch in front of me.

So protective.

My heart clamors in my chest, begging me to give everything to him, and yet unable to. I feel like I'm standing on a precipice, teetering on the edge. But fear holds me back from taking that final step.

"I'm just nervous about today." I touch his cheek, and he leans into my hand.

"I told you, you have nothing to worry about. Becca took care of it. The Sullivans won't be there." He takes my hands and places a gentle kiss on each knuckle.

Strength and warmth.

The possessive looks he gives me eases my anxiety, the way it always does when he lays claim to me. Making me believe that everything will be all right. That maybe I'm not fooling myself trusting that this thing between us is something real, something lasting.

"I'll make us breakfast," Henry says, brushing his lips over mine, before standing.

I give a small nod and wait until he's left the room to make my way to the bathroom, still dizzy and slightly nauseous.

I've felt off for the past couple of days. I've blamed it on nerves, on the stress of everything that's happened with Drew, but there's a nagging feeling in the back of my mind that it's something more. Something I don't even want to contemplate.

Leaning against the bathroom counter, I stare at my reflection, and my heartrate accelerates at the word that flashes like a neon sign in my mind – *pregnant*.

I clench my teeth and avert my gaze. Shit. I count the days in my mind and curse under my breath.

Two, maybe three, days late.

I can't be. But even as I think it, I know it's a probability. Fuck. How could I have been so stupid? I place my hand over my stomach and close my eyes.

What would Henry think? That I planned on trapping him with a child he doesn't want. Just like my mother, believing that a baby would make him mine.

But he's already yours, a small voice in the back of my mind protests.

I shake my head, unable to believe it. Still not willing to take the chance that someone like Henry could really love me. The tape that's been holding my broken heart together all these years threatens to come undone. What would happen if I let it shatter all around me?

Maybe my mind would just go, like Drew and Abby.

No. I'm stronger than that. At least I use to be. Before Henry. Before hope.

Numbly, I step in the shower and turn the water on cold, needing the painful prick of the ice water to clear my head.

Don't panic until you have reason to, I remind myself.

But Drew's words continue to echo like a broken record,

You're just like our mother – a whore.

My heart thuds violently in my chest.

Despite Henry's insistence that what we have is real, I can't shake the feeling that I'm repeating the same cycle. *Like mother, like daughter.*

Chapter 24

Henry

I'm worried about Keeley. Hell, I'm always worried about her. But she's acting more distant than normal, and I can't shake the feeling that she's going to run.

She hasn't spoken about Drew since the day at the café, dismissing me whenever I mention him. I've given her space, but I'm starting to wonder if I should have pushed more, because she's shutting down on me and there's nothing I can fucking do about it.

It's only when my hands are on her skin, my cock buried deep inside her that she lets her guard down. The rest of the time she's constructed a barricade so wide, I don't know if I'll ever be able to bridge the gap.

After the wedding I plan on taking a few weeks off, get her out of the city, away from the reminder of all the shit she's been going through.

My cell vibrates, letting me know that a car is waiting for us.

Unease winds through me. I'm still not happy about this marriage, but I've come to terms that it's what Becca wants.

Keeley walks out of the bedroom and I'm rendered speechless. She's always beautiful. Christ, she could wear a brown paper bag and still be the most gorgeous woman in the world. But dressed in the soft blue silk dress, with matching stilettos, her hair pulled seductively on top of her head in an elegant up-do, she looks like she belongs on the cover of a fucking magazine.

"Is it okay?" she asks, glancing down at the dress. Her chin trembles slightly when her gaze catches mine.

"You're stunning."

"It's too much."

"Don't do that." I move towards her, reaching out and cupping her chin. "Don't act like you're not worthy." I reach into my pocket and pull out the black rectangular box from my pocket and hand it to her. "I thought this would match your dress."

"What is it?" She frowns.

"Open it and see."

Slowly, she cracks the box, eyes widening when she looks down at the diamond and sapphire necklace. On a sigh her mouth parts, and she runs her fingers over the jewels.

"It's beautiful." She shakes her head, then closes the box and hands it back to me. "But I can't."

"Yes, you can." I unhook the necklace and move behind her, placing it around her neck, then fasten the clasp. My fingers brush along her collar bone, and up along her jaw, and I breathe softly in her ear, "This is just the first of many things I'm going to give you."

I feel her tremble against me, and smile, knowing that my touch will always overpower her protests.

Turning her in my arms, I grin down at her, and trace the curve of the necklace.

"Perfect. Just like I thought." I lean in and kiss her gently, eliciting chills. "I had another piece of jewelry that I wanted to give you, but it'll have to wait."

She blinks up at me confused. "I don't want anything else."

I pray to God that's not true. But it's why the five carat engagement ring I purchased last week will stay in my pocket – until I know she's ready. I just hope it's sooner than later, because I want nothing more than to make her my wife.

Chapter 25

Keeley

"Keeley." Becca's face lights up when she sees me. Ignoring the protests of the woman fussing over her, she pulls me into a hug. When she pulls back, she blinks through the tears that threaten to fall. "Sorry. I'm so emotional."

"You look beautiful." And she does. The white, strapless gown is unlike anything I've ever seen. I don't even want to think about what it cost. I heard Henry mumbling over numbers, and nearly choked when he said something about her going three hundred thousand over budget.

The three women, all dressed in lavender bridesmaids' dresses, move to the opposite side of the room, drinking champagne and gossiping over names I've never heard of.

Becca's fingers tremble when she hands me a glass of champagne. I take it and clink the edge with hers.

"I'm doing the right thing," she says, and I can't tell if it's a statement or a question. But I hear the uncertainty in her voice. She sinks slowly into a chair, and takes a deep gulp of the sparkling liquid.

I wonder now if Henry is right. If she isn't marrying him just so that she can have access to the money her father left her. But why throw away a lifetime of happiness for money?

"Do you love him?" I cringe inwardly the moment I ask the question. "Sorry. I shouldn't have asked that."

Dark eyes rest on me and there's a sadness there that I hadn't seen before. "He's a good guy. He'll be a good husband. A good father."

"That's not the same thing," I say softly.

"It's close enough." She straightens her shoulders, her expression suddenly stoic. "Something is better than nothing, right?"

"I guess," I say, not agreeing, but also knowing it's not my place to argue. Who am I to give relationship advice?

There's a small knock on the door, and Henry pokes his head in. "Is everyone decent?"

"Yes." Becca's face lights up again, and she stands and crosses the room towards her brother.

"You look stunning," he says, leaning down to kiss her on the cheek.

"Ready to give me away?" she asks.

Henry sighs and shoves his hands in his pocket. "You still want to go through with this?"

She smacks him lightly on the shoulder and they both laugh, but I can see the tension that lingers in the unanswered question.

"I should go and find my seat," I say, squeezing Becca's hand when I pass by. "Good luck."

She gives me the first genuine smile I've seen, and says, "Just think. It'll be you next."

"Becca." Her name is a low rumble on his lips. So quiet, but the effect hits me with the force of a sonic boom.

Silence follows, tension quickly filling the small room.

Henry glowers at Becca, and she shrinks back.

I don't need an interpreter to understand what passes between them.

Like a punch to the gut, I feel the air leave me in a solid rush. I don't know why I'm so surprised. I'm not marriage material. Not for someone like him.

What had Jax said?

You think that Henry Caldwell would be with someone like you if it wasn't for some gain? Sure, you're a good fuck, but there's never been much in that pretty little head of yours.

The bridesmaids must have caught the awkward conversation, because soft chuckles echo across the room.

My heart immediately sinks in my chest, the truth of how he sees me finally clear. Of course he'd never marry me. I hadn't even begun to hope for such a thing. But to see the anger in his eyes when Becca suggested it, is too much.

Becca pales, concern flashing on her pretty face. "I'm sorry, I just thought–"

"You said enough," Henry barks out, silencing her.

"It's fine," I say, a little too quickly. "I really should go. You look beautiful, Becca."

I rush from the room, blinking back tears of humiliation.

"Keeley, wait," Henry's deep voice commands, stopping me before I make it halfway down the hall.

He stalks towards me, eyes flashing with concern, the anger from the moment before gone.

"You don't understand—"

"And you don't owe me an explanation." I straighten my spine, steeling my emotions. "I've told you, I don't expect anything from you. This thing between us, it's just an overextended one-night stand."

"Don't."

"Don't what? Be honest?"

"Don't trivialize what we have because you're hurt." He reaches out and brushes his knuckles across my cheek. "I love—"

"No. You're confusing lust with love." I take a quick step back, knowing that if I let him touch me, I'll lose my resolve. "That's all this is, all it will ever be. Let's stop pretending it's anything more."

His eyes darken and the muscles in his face tighten.

"You're pushing me away because you're scared."

"I'm pushing you away because it's the right thing to do. If you care about me at all, you'd let me go now, while I still have a fragment of my heart."

"If you'd let me explain—"

"I told you. I understand. I'm not angry with you. But I can't keep doing this. I won't be like her."

"Like who? Like your mother? Is that how you see yourself, see me? You think I would abandon you like that bastard?"

"I don't know, but I can't take the chance."

A wounded look that nearly unravels me crosses his face, as if I've just delivered a death blow.

"Five minutes," a man says from the far side of the hallway.

"Shit." Henry rakes his fingers through his hair, then points at me. "We'll talk about this later."

"There's nothing to talk about. I'll stay for the ceremony, but I think it's best we end this now. I'll get my stuff and be out of your apartment before you get home."

I don't wait for his response, I turn on my heels and race towards the exit, holding back the sob that threatens to choke me. One glance over my shoulder and I know he doesn't follow.

Relief and regret war inside of me.

I hurt him. I saw it in his eyes.

Pain twists my insides. I shouldn't have said the things I did. But better to leave now, before things get any more complicated. *Like me having his baby.*

Chapter 26

Keeley

I feel my heart shattering in my chest as I make my way through the long corridors.

There's a burning sensation deep within me, and I press my palm to my chest and push at the pain, unable to catch a full breath. The throbbing ache is almost unbearable.

My vision clouds with moisture. I shouldn't have run. I made a promise that I wouldn't. But Henry was right. I'm scared. Terrified. But the more distance I place between us, I don't know what I'm more frightened of, having my heart broken or not being with him.

I hate that I'm pushing him away, when all I really want to do is wrap my arms around him, bury my face in his chest, and hear his deep, rich voice reassure me that everything will be okay.

Not looking where I'm going, I collide with a hard body as I turn the corner. Large hands grab my arms, steadying me.

"I'm sorry," I mutter, pulling away, but the hands don't release me, and when I glance up, I'm staring into shocked blue eyes. I suck in a razor-sharp breath and freeze as a cold chill slides down my spine. It's been years since I've seen his face, but I recognize him instantly. *My father.*

"What are you doing here?" Anger and alarm taint John Sullivans words, as he pulls me around the corner and away from the crowd of people filing into the room where the ceremony is to be held.

"Let go of me." I peel his fingers off my arm.

"I asked you a question." His nostrils flare, every deep-set line in his face clear. A face I'd hoped never to see again.

"You know who I am?" My body vibrates with energy. Rage rather than fear rushes through me. Pure, all-consuming rage, that blazes through me like a wildfire.

"Of course I do. You think I haven't kept an eye on you and your brother after that shit he pulled a couple years ago." He leans into me, face red, eyes furious. "If you think you've come here to humiliate me—"

"You weren't supposed to be here. I would never have come if I'd known."

"Bullshit." His face is pinched, and he gives a harsh, disbelieving shake of his head.

It's then that I see it. Etched in the curve of his lip, the disdain in his eyes, a belief that I'm unworthy of him. I remember that look. It's the same look he gave my mother every time she begged for more.

171

"Why?" Hatred thuds through my veins. "What were we to you? What was she? Just a casual screw, or did you love her?"

"Lower your voice."

"No. I can't imagine you've ever loved anyone but yourself. Was there any guilt, when you found out what she did? Did you ever blame yourself that your child and its mother were dead because of you?"

His face blazes with fury. "The woman was insane. I'm not responsible for what she did."

"She begged you. Came to you and told you how desperate she was. I was there that day, when you tossed her away like garbage."

"You want more money? Is that it?" The accusation is thick, coated with malice.

"More?" Something sinks inside my chest. "I've never taken anything from you."

His hard eyes glint with something spiteful.

"Your brother signed a contract two years ago saying he'd never contact me again. The money he received–"

"You gave Drew money?" Bile burns my throat, souring in my stomach as I swallow it down.

What else don't I know?

He chuckles darkly. "Half a million dollars. Looks like the greedy little bastard played us both."

No. Nausea swelled and a rush of dizziness hits me.

"I've paid the price for my sins. Now it's time for you to leave before I call the police and have you carted out of here with a restraining order."

"Your sins?" Overwhelming emotions slam into me. Anger. Grief. Outrage. "Is that what we are? What Lily was?" I steel my spine and fist my fingers at my side.

He looks at me coldly, nothing but spite in his gaze. No regret for a family he destroyed. Just concern for himself.

I'd always known the man was a monster, abandoning us the way he did. But I never imagined anyone could be so completely remorseless.

"I feel sorry for people like you." I'm trembling, but I clench my jaw, not willing to show him the pain he's caused. I push past him, and he grabs my wrist, but this time his large fingers crush down brutally.

"I don't know what game you're playing, but you can't stay here." He pushes me towards the exit, like he's ready to throw me out of the building. "The minute my wife sees your face, she'll ask questions."

People are looking at us now.

"Because I look like Abby," I sneer.

The color drains from his face.

A bitter laugh tickles my throat. "I know all about her. Seems like it wasn't just us you were a shitty father to."

I barely register his hand, before it cuts across my cheek in a stinging slap.

"John," a woman's small voice echoes behind us. "What's going on?"

The color drains from the man's face, and he turns, shielding me from the woman's sight.

"You'll regret this," he hisses, releasing me.

"John?" The woman's voice is shrill.

"Just business, darling." He turns her away from me, but not before I see her eyes widen as her gaze lands on me. But she's quickly guided away through the large double doors, despite her audible protests.

My face throbs, and blood stains my fingers when I touch my lip. I stand there. Shocked. My cheek burning, mind racing. Old, unrelenting pain stabs like an icepick at my heart, and a numbness settles over me.

I swallow the unpleasant taste in my mouth, unable to move.

"Miss. Are you okay?" A younger man dressed in a tux tilts his head towards me, brows furrowed.

Shakily, I exhale the breath that I've been holding in, and blink at him.

"They're going to be starting the ceremony soon. If you'd like to take your seat, I'll–"

"Thank you, but I'm not feeling well. I'm going to get some air."

With slow, deliberate steps, I walk through the atrium and out the large wooden doors towards the front garden.

I find a bench and sit down heavily, gathering my thoughts. Twisted memories slam my mind, pouring into me like poison. A childhood polluted by anger and abuse that no one should ever have to endure.

Bitterness threatens to cripple me, to eat away at my last ounce of hope.

How much rejection can one person endure?

Like a beacon in the abyss, one memory sustains. *My dark-haired boy, and his promise to find me, to protect me*. It was the first time I'd believed that there was something other than darkness in the world. *Henry*. My knight. My protector. My champion.

A small laugh builds in my throat as I realize that he's still all those things.

Guilt clutches at my throat for insinuating that he was anything like my father. I don't know all of his secrets, and maybe I never will, but I know *him*.

And...*I know I love him*.

The fortress I built around my heart was shattered the moment he touched me. I've just been too scared to allow him to claim it fully. My chest is pressed full with the emotion that grips me.

Love.

Trust.

I'm ready to give the last broken pieces to him.

No more fear.

Gathering my courage, I take a deep breath and start to stand. I have to go to him, make things right.

A hand, warm and large, rests on my shoulder stopping me, and I release a shuddering breath.

Henry. But the weight isn't right, and there's no heated energy pulsing from the touch. Unease flashed and fired at my nerves, and I feel the shift in the air. *Danger*.

Slowly I turn, looking over my shoulder, knowing in that split second that I am one hundred and ten percent screwed.

Jax tilts his head, a terrifying smile playing across his lips. "Now, where do you think you're going, princess?"

Chapter 27

Henry

From the back of the hall, I scan the crowd for any sign of Keeley, and curse under my breath when I don't see her.

"What's wrong?" Becca asks, placing her arm in mine as the first bridesmaid starts down the aisle.

"Nothing. Are you ready?"

She gives a nervous little smile, and fidgets with the bouquet she's holding.

"Do you see Keeley?" Becca stretches her neck, peering into the hall. "I hope she's not upset with me for ruining the surprise. When you told me you bought the ring I thought you'd already asked her." She looks out into the crowded room and she sucks in a breath. "Oh no."

"What?" A knot forms in the pit of my stomach at the look of horror on Becca's face.

"The Sullivans are here," she whispers, her voice tight.

I follow her gaze, catching a glimpse of John's profile.

"You told me Asher uninvited them."

"He did." She licks her lips. "I mean, he told me he did. Why would he lie?"

"Dammit, Becca."

One of her bridesmaid's raises an eyebrow at me.

I shake my head and try to hold back my anger. It's her fucking wedding day, but all I can see is red.

"What are we going to do?" she asks.

I have no fucking clue. My first instinct is to find Keeley and get her the hell out of here.

The last of the bridesmaids starts her walk down the aisle.

The music cues. Becca places her hand on top of mine and with clear tension between us, we start our walk to the front of the hall, where the weasely looking Asher waits with a smirk-like grin plastered on his face.

There's still no sign of Keeley. Where the hell is she? Did she see Sullivan and leave? A million scenarios, all ending in me putting my fist through the man's face, run through my mind.

"I'm really sorry, Henry," Becca whispers through the fake smile she gives the onlookers.

"We'll talk about it later."

"I'd never hurt you, or Keeley. Not on purpose." Emotion chokes her words and she looks as if she's ready to break down.

"I know. It'll be all right."

She nods and blinks away tears.

When we reach the front, the minister steps forward and asks, "Who gives this woman to be married to this man?"

I glance at Asher, the same uneasy feeling creeping into my chest as it always does when I'm around him. The man seems to be gloating. I wince and feel an animal-like growl stir in my chest.

"Henry?" Becca says softly, when I don't answer the minister's question.

I look down at her, holding her gaze. *My baby sister*. The overprotective brother in me hangs close to the surface, ready if she says the word, to call the whole wedding off.

"I want you to be happy," I say, low enough that only she can hear.

"I will be."

I don't know if I believe her, or even if she believes it herself, but this is what she wants, and I won't stand in her way.

With a heavy sigh, I nod, and turn back towards the minister.

A ripple of foreboding clenches my gut. Some primal instinct that tells me something is wrong.

Keeley.

"Henry." Becca nudges me.

I'm about to say the words when the room explodes in chaos.

Someone shouts. A shot fires, shattering one of the crystal chandeliers above, and sending tiny pieces of glass raining down on the people below.

Asher dives behind Becca, using her like a shield.

I shove him away, pulling Becca behind me, and guiding her behind the large wooden altar.

People are screaming, racing to the exits, and all I can think about is Keeley.

Fuck. I knew something was wrong. Felt it in my chest. I should have gone after her. I don't know what the hell is happening, but I have no doubt she's involved.

"Stay here," I order.

"Henry, wait." She grabs at my sleeve.

"I have to find Keeley."

She gives a small nod, and lets me go.

Crouching low, I move around the altar, scanning the room.

Where is she?

Awareness, like a tiny prick at my consciousness pulls my gaze to her, and the hairs on the back of my neck stand on end.

Even from this distance I can see that her lip is swollen and bleeding. I'm going to kill whoever put their hands on her.

I see the gunman then.

Chills skate across my skin.

Standing in the shadows, dark hoodie pulled over his head, I recognize him from the pictures Michael sent me.

Drew.

His weapon is trained on another man, kneeling in front of him, hands on the back of his head.

Shit. It's John Sullivan. His wife Sarah is beside him, crying hysterically.

"Shut up, or I'll shut you up," Drew screams, pointing the gun at the small, middle-aged woman, who visibly shrinks at the threat.

"She hasn't done anything," Keeley pleads. "Let her go. Let them both go before this goes any further.

You don't have to do this. We can leave now, before–
"

Drew mumbles something that I can't hear, but whatever it is I see Keeley pale, then her gaze darts around the room until she finds me. The terror in that single look undoes me. What the fuck did he say to her?

When I start towards them, Keeley shakes her head for me to stop, and I see her mouth the word, *run*.

Like fucking hell, I will.

"Put the weapon down, Drew." The command is halting, even to my own ears, and I see the kid hesitate briefly, before redirecting his aim at me.

"Stay back."

Darts of fear pierce me. But not for myself. For Keeley.

"You don't have to do this. I know you're in trouble, but there're other ways to solve the problem. Let me help you."

"Help me. Like you've helped Keeley, by turning her into a whore like our mother."

I see Keeley flinch, and it takes all my strength not to tear into the little bastard.

"I love your sister, that's why I want to help you."

"Bullshit. You're just like him." Drew points the gun back at John.

"We had a deal," John hisses.

"You're deal is shit. I want more. And you're going to give it to me."

"What's your plan, Drew?" I ask, taking slow, even steps towards him. "As soon as you fired that shot, someone called the police. The entire place will be surrounded within minutes."

"Stop talking," Drew hits his head repeatedly. "I can't think when you're talking." He points the gun at Keeley and I swear my heart stops in my chest. "Make him stop talking, or I will."

"Okay." She gives me a sidelong glance. "He'll stop. Just tell us what you want. Because I know you don't want to hurt anyone."

"You don't know what I want," he screams, pointing the gun wildly between us.

"Then tell me." Keeley puts her hands up, and I don't know how she keeps her composure. But her voice stays calm, steady. "Tell me what you want."

"I want him to pay, to suffer like we suffered." With rage in his eyes, Drew marches towards John, and with the heel of his boot, kicks the man in the face.

John falls backwards, blood instantly gushing from his nose, now bent unnaturally.

"Drew. I know you're angry. So am I. But this isn't going to fix anything."

"Listen to your sister, kid," John bites out, spitting blood.

"You don't get to speak." Drew jams the barrel of the gun into the man's temple, then takes a step back, eyes wild and frantic. He runs a tattooed hand through unruly brown hair, then glances around the room as if looking for someone. "I can't. Can't do this."

"You don't have to." My heart nearly stops when Keeley takes a step towards him.

Air rasped from my lungs. I want to scream at her to stay back, but she just keeps moving towards him.

"Please, Drew. You know how this will end."

John stands unsteadily, and wipes the blood from his face. He's bigger than the kid by three or four inches, and outweighs him by a good fifty pounds. At full height, John Sullivan is a powerful and intimidating man, and Drew visibly shrinks back.

"You won't shoot me. Will you, son? Now give me the weapon before anyone gets hurt. We can pretend this whole thing never happened."

For a moment, I actually think the kid might hand over the weapon. Then like a caged animal, Drew shrieks. A pained and crazed sound that shreds my senses.

Both Keeley and John draw back, and I take the moment to rush towards Keeley, pulling her behind me.

Drew keeps screaming, eyes closed on whatever demon is torturing his soul.

"Go. Get out of here," I say harshly between gritted teeth. "I'll deal with your brother."

"I can't." She shakes her head franticly. "Please, just go before–"

"Before what, princess?" A grizzly laugh echoes through the hall. "Did you really think I'd let him walk out of here?" Jax moves from the shadows, gun trained on me. "No. I think it's time we all had a little heart to heart."

Real fear seizes me when I see the look in his eyes. Eyes just as wild and crazed as Drew's. Worse. Because there's also an emptiness in them, a void.

Fear slicks my flesh, clammy and cold, because I see it in his eyes – he has no intention of letting *any of us* leave here alive.

Chapter 28

Keeley

Jax's bitter laughter bleeds through the room, making my stomach heave.

"You." Recognition and disdain cross my father's face.

Jax chuckles sadistically, eyes raging with the thirst of revenge. "You remember me. Good. I was worried you'd forgotten."

"This is who you're working with?" My father's eyes bulge and he looks at me accusingly.

"No." My throat constricts to the point that I don't know how I'm getting any air into my lungs.

"Keeley has nothing to do with this asshole," Henry bites out.

"That's not exactly true, is it princess?" Jax smiles, eyes so dark I swear I can see the fires of hell burning there.

"Screw you."

"Oh I plan on it."

The threat is clear and I feel Henry's entire body tense.

I gulp around the fear and guilt in my throat. This is my fault. I'm the one that brought Henry into this.

And I'm the one who has to stop it.

"Fine. You want me." I maneuver around Henry so quickly he doesn't have time to react. Face to face with Jax, the barrel of his gun inches from my face, I glare up at him. "Then let's go. No one has to get hurt."

"Keeley." Henry's pained growl sends chills racing down my spine.

I ignore him, locking my gaze on Jax, who just smirks, then begins to circle me, trailing his gun over my shoulder, across my breasts. Unable to control the shiver that races down my spine, I grit my teeth.

"I'm yours. Just let them go."

"You think that's what this is about?" The cold edge of the gun snakes under my hair, along my neck, then he jerks me back against his chest, barrel digging deep into my temple. "You weren't that good of a fuck, darling. This is about me and your Daddy. Isn't it John?"

Drew lets out a pathetic snivel and starts rocking from one foot to the other. "He has to pay."

"Make the call, John," Jax says, pulling a phone from his pocket, and pressing a series of numbers. "Your men have the details. They just need your password."

My father catches the device when Jax throws it to him. "And if I say no?"

"Then you all die."

Sirens blare in the distance.

"He has to pay," Drew repeats in a monotonous tone. His mind is gone, eyes blank. "He has to pay."

Drew's weapon hangs limply in his hand, and I see Henry's gaze trained on it, on him. Henry inches forward, intent in his eyes.

Jax must see it too, because he turns his gun on Henry.

"Let's not be a hero, Caldwell." One large arm tightens around me, and with the other hand Jax pulls back the hammer of the gun. "We all know where that got you last time. Taking the heat for another man's mistake. Fucking pathetic."

Henry's eyes widen just slightly, and his nostrils flare. "How the fuck do you know about that?"

"Why don't you tell him, John?" He snickers sadistically. The bastard is enjoying this.

I glance at my father and see the first signs of guilt etched across his face. He pushes out a weighted breath and rakes a hand over his eyes, then through his silvering hair.

"Come on, you can say it. I knocked up your little girl. Fucked her till she squealed like a pig. She was a beauty." Jax sucks on his teeth, then chuckles. "Too bad she was bat-shit crazy."

It takes me a moment to realize he's talking about Abby.

I see horror in Henry's eyes and it hits me hard, the secret he's kept. That he'd allowed people to believe he'd been the one responsible. For Abby's pregnancy. For her depression. Her death. *Why?*

Sirens scream louder.

"You knew?" The grief and anger coming off Henry is almost tangible, but it's directed at my father.

I can't see Jax's face, but I can hear the smirk in his voice. "Of course he knew. But he made sure no one else did. Isn't that right, Sullivan? Couldn't have people thinking that your sweet little angel was tramping around with scum like me."

A small sound comes from the corner. *Sarah.* The poor woman looks like she's about to pass out. Like me, she's only a victim in the web of lies. Deceived by the man who was supposed to protect her.

Pain. Betrayal. Hatred. The remnants of sin swirls around the room, leaving no one untouched.

"Why are you doing this, Jax?" My insides twist painfully. "What do you want?"

"Money, darling." His nose is in my hair, and he breathes in deeply. "And a little bit of revenge. See Daddy dearest over there fucked me over pretty good. He couldn't put anything on me for just screwing his little princess, so he had shit planted on me. Spent a year in juvie, two in State. For what? Knocking up a crazy chick?"

"I'll see you rot in prison for the rest of your life," John scowls.

"You won't see anything, unless you transfer those funds." Jax nods at Drew. "You've got twenty seconds or your son puts a bullet in your wife's head."

Wild and crazed, Drew point his gun at Sarah.

"John." Her eyes are wide, terrified.

"All right," he grounds out through clenched teeth. Face red, nostrils flared, he makes the call. The entire transaction takes less than a minute. "It's done."

Drew pulls a phone from his pocket, then nods. "The funds have been transferred."

"You got what you want, now let Keeley go." Henry's voice is deathly quiet.

Jax scoffs out a laugh, and starts to walk backwards, pulling me with him.

"I don't think so. I'm going to need a little insurance." He drags me towards a service door. "You know what to do kid. Here's your chance for revenge."

"I can't." Drew lifts his gun, hand shaking uncontrollably. He glances over at me, and I see a glimpse of the boy he once was. Scared. Alone. Vulnerable.

"Drew, please. You can stop this."

"Do it," Jax hollers.

Drew twitches, his breathing ragged, moisture gathering in his eyes.

"Even if you kill us, you still have to walk through those doors." Henry's voice is low, calm, as if speaking to a wild animal. "Only you'll be facing murder charges."

"The only people who've seen me are in this room." Jax's breathing is hot and heavy in my ear. "Now take the shot, Drew."

He's planning on using Drew as a scapegoat. That's his only way out. *Shit.*

"Think about what you're doing, Drew" I beg. "He's not going to let any of us leave here alive."

Drew looks at me, then at Jax.

"You're going to listen to your whoring sister, or me. I've got your back, kid. Just take the shots."

Drew lifts his gun and I know he's going to do it. There's murder in his eyes.

I bite down hard on Jax's hand, tasting blood. Fighting him off, I rush towards Drew, just as he pulls back on the trigger.

We both tumble to the floor, and the shot goes wide.

"Fucking bitch," Jax curses, raising his gun at me and I know I'm going to die.

Doors crash open and the room suddenly fills with police.

"Put your weapon down," someone orders.

Jax smirks one last time. "See you in hell, princess."

Everything happens so quickly, I barely register Henry rushing towards me, or the shots fired. The next thing I know, I'm on my back, Henry's heavy body covering mine.

Liquid warmth spreads across my chest.

I can't breathe.

I'm sure I've been shot.

But there's no pain.

Henry groans, lifting up on one arm so that his weight releases me slightly. His hands are on me, checking for injury.

"You're okay?" Henry cups my chin, and forces me to look at him. His body is still heavy on top of me, shielding me from the chaos that resumes around us.

People are screaming orders, and from the corner of my vision, I see police placing Drew in handcuffs. John sitting with his head in his hands. Sarah crying uncontrollably beside him. Jax's lifeless body lying in a pool of blood, his unseeing eyes locked on me.

I shudder and look away.

"I'm all right," I say breathlessly, placing my hand on Henry's chest. When my hand comes back slick with blood, I freeze. "Oh my God, you've been shot."

He winces and rolls onto his side.

I pull back the black suit and gasp at the amount of blood that covers his once white shirt.

Oh God. No.

"Help." The word is an inaudible whisper, and I have to push the next ones past the large lump in my throat. "Someone help."

Time doesn't move the same way when your heart has been flayed open – there are moments that stand still, others that move so quickly you wonder if they really happened.

Police and paramedics swarm us. Someone tears open Henry's shirt, and I see the bullet wound just below his right shoulder. Blood gushes from it like a geyser.

"Stay with me." Henry reaches for my hand, his grip tight on mine.

"I won't leave you."

His lips twitch up in a small smile, then his face contorts in a spasm of pain.

"Right pocket," he says through clenched teeth, as the paramedics slide a board under him.

I reach into his pocket and pull out a small velvet box. My stomach does a somersault as I realize what it is. I open the box and suck in a breath.

An engagement ring.

A tear slides down my cheek and I brush it away with the back of my hand.

"One, two, three." The paramedics lift Henry onto the gurney.

"Miss, I need you to come with me." A police officer stands in front of me, eyes full of concern.

The paramedics steers the gurney towards the exit.

I shake my head. "I have to go with him. I promised I wouldn't leave."

"We need your statement."

I ignore the officer's protest and rush to Henry's side, taking his hand.

His grasp is weaker than before, his face pale, eyes heavy.

He's going to be okay. He has to be.

"Marry...me," he whispers harshly.

I press my lips against his and nod, but when I pull back his eyes are closed.

"Henry." I squeeze his hand, but he doesn't respond.

"Miss, we need to go."

Releasing him, I stumble back.

The only thing I can think as I watch them wheel him away is, *I never told him I loved him.*

Chapter 29

Keeley

I pace the small hospital waiting room, glancing up at the mechanical clock hanging on the wall, and let out a trembling breath.

"What's taking so long? Someone should have come and told us something by now."

"Sit down." Becca pats the chair beside her, brows furrowed.

"I'm so sorry about all this." I rub the back of my neck wearily and sit down.

"It isn't your fault."

I shrug, knowing she's wrong. "Is Asher coming?"

"I told him not to." A small frown tugs at her lips and she lets out a long sigh. "It's over between us."

I look at her, horrified. Only a few hours ago she was standing at the altar ready to commit her life to him.

More guilt consumes me.

"Don't do that." Becca takes my hand and squeezes it gently. "Don't blame yourself. Asher wasn't right for me. I just didn't want to see it." She sighs and swipes at a tear that falls over her cheek. "But Henry did. God, he can be so controlling. Bossy. Sometimes I forget he only wants to protect me. I should have listened to him."

And because of me, she might lose him.

"You know, when the first bullet fired, Asher actually hid behind me. It was Henry that pulled me down. Made sure I was safe."

"He took a bullet for me." The words don't seem real. "Who does that?"

"Henry."

"Yeah." *My Knight.*

Becca tilts her head, a sad smile curving her lips. "When we were kids, he always had to be the hero, saving me and Abby from some imaginary bad guy. Always the protector."

A memory of a dark-haired boy and his sword flashes in my mind. *My champion. The slayer of dragons.*

"You knew about Abby," I say, already knowing the answer. "That he wasn't the baby's father?"

Becca nods, eyes clouding over in memory.

"When the rumors started, Abby begged him to go along with it. I never really understood why he did. To protect her I guess. But after she…when she took her life, everyone pointed their fingers at Henry. I think he started to believe the accusations. That her death was his fault. There was a long time when I thought I would lose him too…until you."

And now we might both lose him.

My breath catches in my throat and I look away, unable to meet the acceptance in her gaze. I deserve her anger, not her support.

"He's going to be all right." Becca places her hand on my shoulder.

"You don't know that."

"I know my brother. He's a fighter. And he has a lot to live for. He has you."

My fist tightens on the ring box. "He was going to ask me to marry him."

"I know."

"I've never believed in happily ever after. Not until him. And now—" A small sob lodges in my throat.

"Don't let your mind go there. Not until we know what's going on."

I nod, knowing she's right.

"Miss Caldwell?" The muscular, tattooed male nurse that seems to have taken a personal interest in Becca, stands over us, holding two pairs of scrubs.

"Do you have news? Is Henry...is he okay?" My voice cracks on the last word.

"Sorry. I haven't heard anything," he says, blue eyes stoic. "I thought you two might be more comfortable in these.

I glance down at my blood-stained dress and cringe.

Henry's blood.

In the restroom, I lean with my palms on the cold, white ceramic sink, and I glance at my reflection.

A nightmare. That's what this is. A cold, hellish nightmare that I can't wake up from.

"He's going to be all right," I say to my reflection, but there's no certainty in my voice, because nothing in my life is ever all right. Just a chaotic, broken mess.

He was my forever, and yet I was quick to run, to believe the worst in him. Now I may never get the chance to tell him I love him. That I want to be his. To have his child.

God. I touch my stomach. *His baby.*

I didn't realize until now how much I wanted it. To be his wife. Be a family. I was just too scared to admit it. Too afraid to give my heart to someone completely. Afraid that losing him would destroy me.

A humorless laugh escapes my lips.

I was right. The pain is unbearable. But the love he's given me. The acceptance. It's worth the jagged torment that cuts through my heart and soul, leaving me exposed and bare.

One more day.

One more kiss.

One chance to tell him I love him.

Please. I say a silent prayer to whatever god is listening. *I won't be a coward any longer. Just let him live.*

Chapter 30

Henry

Relief swims in the blue eyes that look down on me. The most beautiful eyes I've ever seen. My angel. My Keeley.

"You stayed." My voice is gravelly.

"Of course, I stayed." A single tear rolls over her cheek.

Wires and tubes are attached to my hand when I reach up to touch her face, wiping the moisture away with my knuckles.

What cuts me up is the fear she tries to contain.

"You saved me," she says, holding my palm against her face.

"And you said yes." It's the last thing I remember before I lost consciousness.

"Yes." She hiccups over a sob.

"Hey." I try to sit up, wanting to comfort her, but pain shoots through my shoulder. Fuck. Getting shot hurts like a bitch.

"I'm sorry. I'm okay. I just…" She closes her eyes and takes a few steadying breaths. "I thought I was going to lose you. I…"

"I know, sweetheart." I bring her hand to my lips and kiss each knuckle.

Catching her lip between her teeth, I see her warring with the unsaid sentiment.

"Your brother, is he okay?"

"They took him into custody."

"We'll get him the help he needs." The help Abby should have gotten. Drew's young. With therapy and medication, he may be able to function normally. But one thing is certain, I won't let him anywhere near Keeley, until I'm absolutely sure he won't harm her. Physically, mentally, or emotionally.

She's my first priority. *Always.*

"Sarah, John's wife was here earlier." Keeley brushes her hair behind her ear and glances down at the floor.

"Shit."

"It's okay. She's a victim in all this." Her eyes cloud over slightly.

"What did she want?"

"To hear the truth from me. I don't know if it helped."

Fuck. I wish that I'd been there for her. I don't want her to have to deal with anything alone ever again.

"I'm so sorry." Her voice is broken, ragged, laced with guilt. "For everything."

"None of this is your fault."

"Maybe not. But if you'd never met me—"

"If I'd never met you I'd be lost, broken, missing half of my heart."

"God, I love you," she says on a sigh. Her eyes widen when she realizes what she said.

A lump knots at the base of my throat. "I love you too, Keeley."

"It's enough." She fidgets with something in her hand and I realize it's the ring box.

"What's enough sweetheart?"

"You. Us." Her voice is soft, gaze downcast, and I can tell it takes everything within her to say the words.

I hold my breath, watching as her steel fortress melts away.

Exposed.

Raw.

Brave.

She stands before me, giving me everything – her heart.

I curse the pain that slices through my chest when I reach for her, but I need to hold her.

"You're going to open your wound," she says, when I pull her down beside me.

"I don't care. I need to feel you."

Curling beside me, she rests her head on my good shoulder and mumbles, "Strength and warmth."

"What?"

"When I'm with you the emptiness disappears. The darkness goes away. I promised…" Emotion makes her voice crack. "I swore that if you pulled through this, I wouldn't be afraid anymore."

I hooked my knuckle under her chin, forcing her to look at me.

"It's okay to be afraid sometimes. Shit, when I saw the look in Jax's eye when he had the gun pointed at you...I've never been so fucking scared in my life."

"You saved me."

"I promised I would." I grin. "Just took me twenty years to do it."

She laughs softly.

A warm ache fills my chest.

"I love that sound."

"What?"

"You. Happy."

"You make me happy."

I nuzzle my nose into her hair, and breathe in the sweet scent of her.

Her body stiffens slightly.

"What's wrong?"

"I have to tell you something." There's tension in the words that make the hairs on the back of my neck stand on end.

She tucks her chin into my chest.

"Keeley, look at me."

She winces, but obeys.

"Tell me."

"I had one of the nurses run a blood test. I didn't know, and I wanted to be sure before I told you."

"Are you sick?"

"No. I'm pregnant," she blurts out.

Pregnant?

I choke over the swell of emotion. "Fuck."

"Are you mad?"

"No. God. Of course not. Just shocked." I brush my knuckles over her cheek and study her. I know the fears she's kept locked inside her. "Are *you* okay?"

"Yes." Her eyes cloud for a moment, but just as quickly the brightness returns. "Scared. But in a good way."

Courage. Hope. Love. I see it in her eyes.

I press my lips against hers. Just that small contact and my cock twitches. Desire swells. I'll never get enough of her.

"How long before I'm out of here?"

As if sensing the need stirring within me, she chuckles. "A couple days at least."

"Shit."

"I'll make it up to you…" Her tongue darts out over her bottom lip and the look she gives me makes me groan. "When we get home."

Home. It's the first time she's called it that. I grin down at her and sigh.

Her smile matches my own as she snuggles deeper into my hold, threading her fingers through mine.

"I'm so tired." She yawns. "But I don't want to leave you."

"Close your eyes." It dawns on me that the sky is dark outside my window, the moon high in the sky. My body is washed in fatigue, my eyes heavy. "You can sleep in my arms. Where you belong."

"Henry?" Her voice is light.

"Yeah?"

"I love you."

My chest tightens.

Maybe the bullet pierced more than my shoulder, because if this isn't heaven, I don't know what is.

She's my life now. Every beautiful, broken, part of her.

Mine.

"I love you too, sweetheart."

Epilogue

Keeley

Six years later...

"Mama, mama. Look what Daddy gave me." A whirlwind of dark hair runs into the bedroom and jumps on the bottom of the bed, swinging a wooden sword.

Lily squirms in my arms, chubby fists reaching for her brother.

"My girls are finally awake." Henry saunters into the room, dark hair mussed. Even now, he takes my breath away. His knuckles graze my cheek, before he leans over and kisses my forehead, eyes filled with an emotion only reserved for me.

Warmth and strength.

Harrison drops to his knees beside me and holds out the old wooden sword. "Look Mama."

"I see." I gaze at my beautiful boy. Already so big and so much like his father.

"I'm going to be a knight and fight dragons."

"Like your daddy."

Harrison tilts his head and blinks up at Henry, eyes wide. "You were a knight?"

"The bravest," I say.

Henry sits beside me on the bed and wraps an arm behind my shoulder, so that my back is resting against his chest.

"I'm going to be brave too," Harrison says, giving me a toothless grin. "And keep you and Lily safe, cause that's what knights do, right Daddy?"

A soft chuckle rumbles from his throat. "That's right. We fight for love. That's what makes a hero."

Harrison grins so wide I feel it right in the center of my chest.

My little knight.

Lily babbles and crawls to Harrison. He makes a funny face and she gives a full-chested baby laugh.

Love. It's the most precious gift.

I never thought it was possible to love so much, to be loved.

Henry threads his fingers with mine and nuzzles his nose in my hair.

"So damn, beautiful," he whispers, sending a thrill down my spine.

My champion.

My hero.

My husband.

I never imagined life could be more than just surviving. But it's so much more. *Love is living.*

And I have more love than any person deserves.

There are some wounds that still haunt me, maybe always will. But no one survives a battle without a few scars.

I smile and glance around at my family, heart full.
Fairy tales do exist.
Sometimes you just have to fight a few dragons to get your happily ever after.

About the Author

C.M. Seabrook is the author of Fighting Blind, Moody, and Melting Steel, as well as the Amazon bestselling fantasy romance Cara's Twelve, as well as the Therian Agents Paranormal Romance Series, and co-author of the Mated by Magic series.

When she isn't reading or writing sexy stories, she's most likely spending time with her family, cooking, singing, or racing between soccer, hockey and karate practices. She's living her own happily ever after with her husband of fifteen years and their two daughters.

She loves creating new exciting characters - from sexy, bad boy alphas, to the passionate, fiery women who love them.

Canadian born and bred, she started life in Edmonton, Alberta, and now resides in London, Ontario. She attended Western University where she graduated with an Honors degree in Anthropology.

Her guilty pleasures include red wine, pasta, binge watching Starz originals, and hanging out with her rescue pup, Jaxx.

She loves to hear from her readers and can be reached at cm.seabrook.books@gmail.com

SIGN UP FOR C.M. Seabrook's NEWSLETTER FOR LATEST NEWS!
https://app.mailerlite.com/webforms/landing/r8p4k2

18225909R00115

Printed in Great Britain
by Amazon